LEGACY

THE MCBRIDE CHRONICLES
BOOK THREE

"The legacy of heroes is the memory of a great name."

Benjamin Disraeli
(1804-1881)

VALERIE GREEN

Legacy

a novel

THE MCBRIDE CHRONICLES
BOOK THREE

hancock
house

Copyright © 2023 Valerie Green

Cataloguing data available from Library and Archives Canada
978-0-88839-766-9 [paperback]
978-0-88839-767-6 [epub]

FRONT/BACK COVER DESIGN: J. RADE

FRONT COVER ARTWORK: Shutterstock

PRODUCTION & DESIGN: J. Rade

EDITOR: D. MARTENS

We acknowledge the support of the Government of Canada through the Canada Book Fund and the Canada Council for the Arts, and of the Province of British Columbia through the British Columbia Arts Council and the Book Publishing Tax Credit.

Hancock House gratefully acknowledges the Halkomelem Speaking Peoples whose unceded, shared and asserted traditional territories our offices reside upon.

Published simultaneously in Canada and the United States by
HANCOCK HOUSE PUBLISHERS LTD.

19313 Zero Avenue, Surrey, B.C. Canada V3Z 9R9

#104-4550 Birch Bay-Lynden Rd, Blaine, WA, U.S.A. 98230-9436

(800) 938-1114   Fax (800) 983-2262

www.hancockhouse.com   info@hancockhouse.com

For my beloved mother Eleanor (Nora) Elizabeth Stofer -
Who always kept the home fires burning.

AUTHOR'S NOTE

The tragedy of two World Wars, a major world flu epidemic in 1918 and the sinking of S.S. *Sophia*—all have a profound effect on the McBride family.

The voice of Sarah's son, Stephen, takes over the story in *Legacy*, with his experiences in World War I and that of his girlfriend, Letty Caldwell. By the end of Part One, matriarch Jane McBride realizes it will be up to her eight-year-old grandson Caleb to continue the legacy of the McBrides.

Part Two begins Caleb's story. Always fascinated with flying from an early age, Cal's life is intertwined with the birth of aeronautics in British Columbia and covers the barnstorming and bush-flying years, leading to him training pilots in World War II.

In Part Three, Caleb enters the war scene in 1941 as a bomber pilot in England. Toward the end of the war, Cal meets Maggie Graham and they fall in love. They plan their wedding and eventual return to Victoria. But fate intervenes and the book concludes with the mystery of who will eventually inherit Providence after Jane's death.

I hope you enjoy reading *Legacy* as much as I have enjoyed writing it and will want to read more in the final book in the series, *Tomorrow*.

Valerie Green, 2023

TABLE OF CONTENTS

THE McBRIDE FAMILY TREE

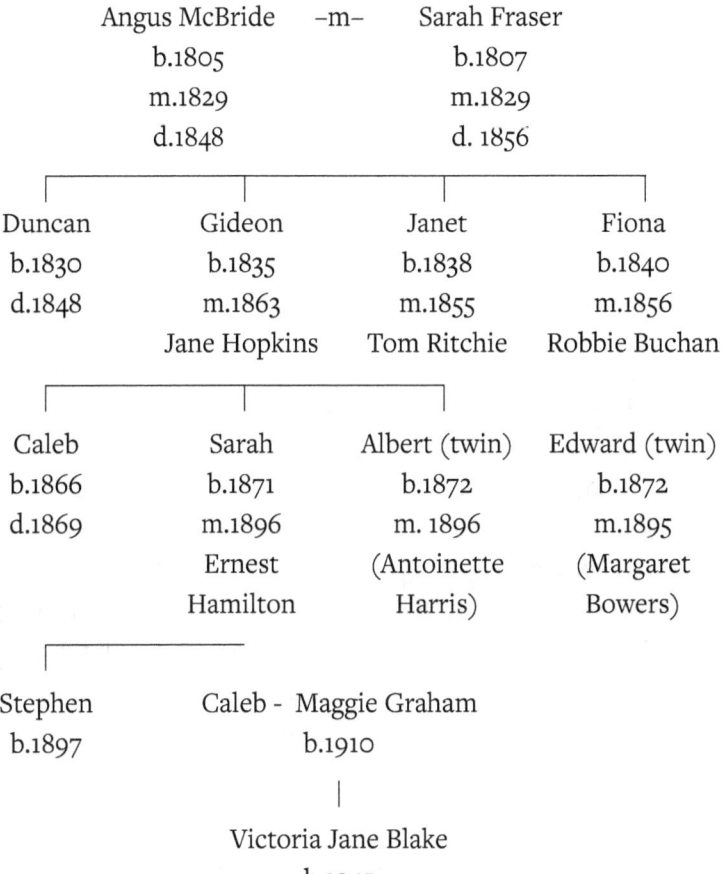

Angus McBride   –m–   Sarah Fraser
b.1805   b.1807
m.1829   m.1829
d.1848   d. 1856

Duncan	Gideon	Janet	Fiona
b.1830	b.1835	b.1838	b.1840
d.1848	m.1863	m.1855	m.1856
	Jane Hopkins	Tom Ritchie	Robbie Buchan

Caleb	Sarah	Albert (twin)	Edward (twin)
b.1866	b.1871	b.1872	b.1872
d.1869	m.1896	m. 1896	m.1895
	Ernest	(Antoinette	(Margaret
	Hamilton	Harris)	Bowers)

Stephen   Caleb - Maggie Graham
b.1897   b.1910

Victoria Jane Blake
b.1945

THE CALDWELL FAMILY TREE

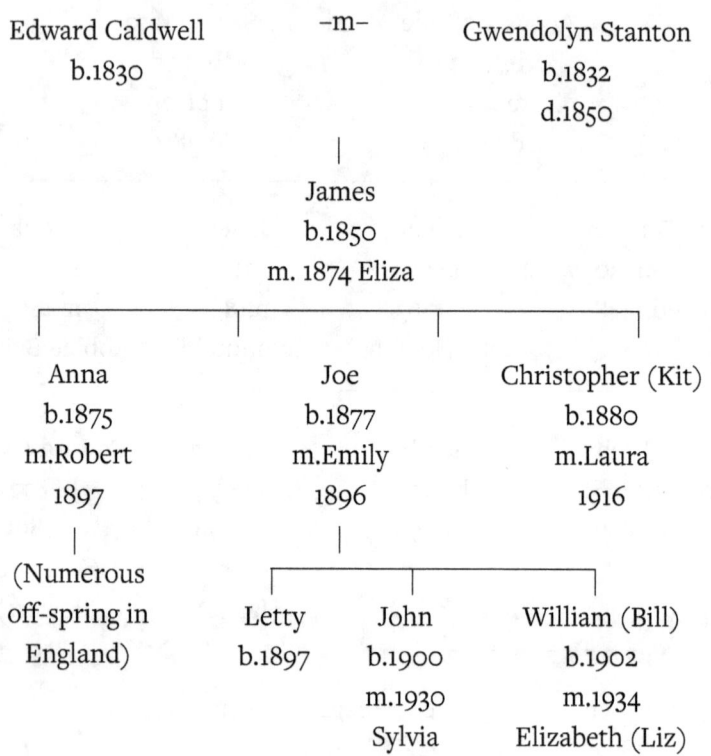

Edward Caldwell   –m–   Gwendolyn Stanton
b.1830   b.1832
                                           d.1850

James
b.1850
m. 1874 Eliza

Anna   Joe   Christopher (Kit)
b.1875   b.1877   b.1880
m.Robert   m.Emily   m.Laura
1897   1896   1916

(Numerous
off-spring in   Letty   John   William (Bill)
England)   b.1897   b.1900   b.1902
                           m.1930   m.1934
                           Sylvia   Elizabeth (Liz)

PART ONE

$\left(1898-1919\right)$

The Clouds of War
STEPHEN

CHAPTER 1

I am told that I was born in the same bed in which my grandmother had given birth to my mother and my two uncles. It was a sort of tradition that McBrides had to be born at Providence, in the master bedroom. Providence was the house my grandparents built in the 1860s. My mother had wanted to continue the tradition, as I was the first McBride grandchild.

Actually I am a Hamilton, not a McBride. My father, Ernest Hamilton, is a successful lawyer who made a great deal of money with wise property investments. After he married my mother, a McBride, he became even wealthier, of course, because the McBrides had pots of money which Grandfather had made from his transportation business and from lucky gold strikes on the Fraser and in the Cariboo. Our own house in the Rockland area of Victoria, known as Hamilton House, was almost as grand as Providence.

Nonetheless, for all the wealth that surrounded us, my mother much preferred the simple things in life, like riding her horse, tending her garden, attending meetings for women's suffrage and helping the poor or abused and abandoned women. She actually did a great deal of hands-on charitable work at hospitals and homes for the needy, and I grew up admiring her tremendously. I also respected her courage and forward-thinking mind. A year after my grandmother purchased an automobile, my mother did the same thing, and the two of them were among the first women to be seen driving those machines through the streets of Victoria. It was very daring for women.

My mother also doted on me, which was an enormous embarrassment, especially as I grew older and had school friends visiting. I was an only child for so many years, so I suppose she was entitled to lavish all her maternal love on me, but nonetheless it did cause me humiliation on numerous occasions. I often retreated next door to the Caldwell house, where I could play with Letitia, William and John, or they would come over and play with me.

I was the first person to call Letitia Caldwell "Letty," much to her annoyance. I still remember that day quite clearly. It was actually one of my first memories of her, and I think we were both about five at the time. Neither of us had yet started school, anyway.

I was playing on my swing, which Father had built in our garden, when suddenly this curly-haired little creature squeezed through the gap in the laurel hedge that separated our two properties.

"What'cha doing, Stevie?" she asked.

"Swingin'."

"Can I swing with you?"

"Nope."

"Why not?"

"Cos you're too young."

"I'm five!"

"Me too."

"Well then ...?"

"Okay." I jumped off and allowed her to sit on the seat before giving her a gentle push.

"Little Letty Caldwell," I said. "Letty ... Letty ... Letty."

"My name is Letitia Ann Caldwell, *not* Letty!" she replied indignantly.

"Well, I shall always call you Letty. It suits you better."

"Does it?"

"Yep ..."

And then, with the typically quick and fleeting minds of children, our attention moved on to something else. I think it was a colourful butterfly that we both attempted to chase and capture as we ran across the lawn together. I also believe that from that day forward, Letty and I were practically inseparable.

I remember hearing my mother cry one day, and this really frightened me. My nanny had taken me for a walk, and when we returned, Granny Mac was waiting for us in the drawing room. She gave me a hug and told me my mother was upstairs dressing and would be down shortly. After Granny Mac left, I ran upstairs ahead of Nanny to find my mother, but before entering her room I heard her crying. Nanny called for me to stop and go to my own room, but instead I barged into my mother's room and threw my arms around her.

"Mama, what's wrong?" I asked. "Why are you crying?"

She dabbed her eyes and hugged me to her breast. "Oh, Stephen dear, it's nothing. I was just ... thinking ... thinking about your ... father ... and what a wonderful man he was."

"But he still *is* wonderful, Mama," I said. "So why are you crying?"

"You're right, Stephen. He still *is* a wonderful man. How silly of me. Come, give Mama a kiss and we'll go downstairs together."

A short time after that incident, my mother and father went abroad for a long holiday. They visited London to see the new king's coronation, and I stayed for part of the time at Providence and part of the time with the Caldwells. Even though I missed my parents, I really rather enjoyed myself during their absence, because everyone spoiled me terribly, especially Granny Mac—that's what I called Grandmother McBride.

All the other children thought she was pretty strict and cold, but she was never that way with me. Although very firm, she was always kind to me, and she and I had many jaunts together in her automobile. By then she had Stapleton, her chauffeur, to drive her around, but she still liked to take the car out herself sometimes. I think she broke the speed limit on a number of occasions, which at that time was five miles per hour, but Granny Mac never was one for abiding by the rules.

Not, that is, until she was back inside Providence and once again became the mistress of her domain. Then, invariably she was aloof and dictatorial and ruled everyone with an iron fist. She always expected the best of people. She told me once that she had had a very hard childhood because she had been so poor, and that I was a very lucky boy to be living in such luxury. But, she added, I must never forget what it was like to be poor.

I wondered on a number of occasions how I could ever forget something that I didn't even remember or know anything about.

CHAPTER 2

After my parents returned from their trip abroad, life continued much the same at Hamilton House. Letty and I were always together. We had been born only two months apart in 1897, and we had so much in common. Our relationship, which started out as best friends, began to change into something else by the time we both turned ten, but neither of us quite knew what.

That was the same year when I found my mother crying again, after Aunt Margaret's funeral. Aunt Margaret was one of my favourite people, and I adored Uncle Teddy also, so when she died we were all devastated, even Granny Mac, who rarely showed her feelings.

My mother kept telling me that it was so unfair because Aunt Bowery, as she called her, was still so young, but she had suffered constantly with an ongoing disease that she had caught in Africa. Although she had never seemed particularly old to me, like Granny Mac or Great Uncle Edward, she also had not seemed very young. She was the same age as my mother, I suppose, which was about thirty-six, but when you're only ten, even thirty-six seems ancient.

I decided that day that I hated funerals because they made everyone so sad. In addition, we all had to wear horrid black outfits and a black armband and then all traipse up to the cemetery at St. Luke's Church on the hill and stand in a circle while Aunt Bowery's body was lowered in a coffin into the earth. It seemed very morbid to me. Letty stood beside me, and during the ceremony she placed her hand in mine and squeezed it tightly. She had tears in her eyes, and that was the day I decided I felt something else for her, more than friendship. I felt like I must always protect her from bad things that happened in life.

I also wrote my first poem that day. It was rather sad, because it was all about death and graveyards filled with dead bodies. I only showed it to Letty, who told me it was very good but far too depressing. However, she understood why I had written it and encouraged me to write more, less sorrowful poems. And so I did.

I also spent a great deal of time with my two uncles. Uncle Teddy was grief stricken for a long time and, according to Granny Mac, was only able to find solace in his work as a doctor. I didn't know what *solace* was, so I looked it up in the dictionary and found it meant comfort and consolation, so my next poem was about comforting people in times of sorrow. I gave it to Uncle Teddy on his birthday the following year.

"You are such a sensitive and talented young fellow," he said. His eyes were very watery as he spoke.

Uncle Bertie, on the other hand, was usually lots of fun and had a dry sense of humour. He loved to play tricks on people, and he laughed a great deal. I heard he had been married once to an awful woman by the name of Antoinette, but I could not remember her because I was just a baby then. All I knew was that he never seemed short of female companionship for any social function we attended, and he seemed to enjoy the company of ladies a great deal.

He encouraged me to visit him at the offices of McBride's Transportation and McBride's Fisheries and said that one day I would probably take over the businesses.

"I don't think I'm cut out to be a businessman like you, Uncle Bertie," I said. "I think I want to be a poet or a great writer one day."

"Well, lad, you certainly have talent in that direction, but you will probably never make much money at it."

"Is money important?" I asked.

He laughed. "Certainly, unless you prefer to starve, and it also helps if you want to live reasonably comfortably."

"You mean you can't live comfortably without money?"

"Oh, I suppose some people manage ... but it is nice to have enough money to really enjoy life."

"I think I would still enjoy life even without money."

"Yes, Stephen, I think you would. You have a great capacity for contentment, and that is a wonderful gift."

Nonetheless, I did like hearing about the businesses that my grandfather had built from scratch. The stories of his glory days as a river boat captain on the Fraser River were colourful and full of adventure, and I wished I had known him, but he had died soon after I was born and I didn't remember him at all.

I'm told he pioneered the waterways and roads of British Columbia, and now Uncle Bertie was becoming equally famous, breaking new ground with McBride's fish canning operations along that same great river. I was proud to be a part of it all, but wondered if it was really what I wanted to do with my life. I wished I had a brother or a sister who might carry on the family tradition, rather than having it all left up to me.

In September of 1910, my wish was granted. I was thirteen years old by then, and finally my parents presented me with a little brother. They christened him Caleb McBride Hamilton and said he was named for a brother of my mother's who had died when he was two years old, before even she was born.

It seemed a rather grand name for such a scrawny little fellow, but undoubtedly he would grow. I hoped that he would live longer than his namesake, so, in order not to tempt fate, I decided instead to always call him Cal.

CHAPTER 3

Victoria experienced a real estate boom over the next few years, and Father bought and sold more property, which made him a great deal of money. He also purchased some acreage at Sooke Lake, and we built a cabin out there where we spent most of our summers. It was a happy time in all our lives, and I decided to call us the Happy Hamiltons, which made Mother and Father laugh.

I liked it best when we took Letty with us out to the lake. She made an awful fuss over little Cal, but I didn't mind, because he was rather special. Those summers were very dear to me and I was inspired to write more poetry, which I put into a small book. I'm sure I must have been a terrific bore to everyone, because I insisted on reading aloud my latest masterpiece of inspirational effort as we all sat around the campfire at night. Mother and Letty never grew tired of hearing my poetry, though, and little Cal was always a captive audience. By the time he was four years old, he followed me everywhere, which was very flattering. I sensed that my father would have preferred me to spend my time in other, more manly pursuits, but nonetheless he always praised me for whatever I did.

By then it was 1914, the year when everyone's life changed. Letty and I were both seventeen, and, although I would describe myself as a somewhat awkward, gangly youth, she had grown into an extremely beautiful young woman. She had the most wonderful, dark, curly hair, which she complained about all the time because it would never stay in place. Her eyes were the deepest blue I had ever seen, and each time I looked into them I felt myself drowning in their liquid beauty. By then, I was desperately in love with her and convinced myself that she felt the same way.

There was talk of war all around the world, so I decided I must inform Letty of my feelings for her, in case I was suddenly whisked away to fight the Germans in Europe and we were parted. The thought of going to battle scared me very much, but I told Granny Mac that I would be more scared of having to live with my conscience if I did not join in the war effort in some way.

"I pray it never comes to you having to make a choice, Stephen," she told me.

My mother, who had spent part of her youth in Germany, joined the conversation, insisting that there would never be a war with Germany.

"We are far too civilized for that," she declared. "And so is Germany. Your Aunt Bowery and I went to a finishing school in Dresden years ago, and we were able to listen to opera and see the world's greatest paintings on display. No, Stephen, I am sure we would never go to war against Germany. All of Europe is far too cultured and enlightened. It would be just too dreadful for words."

But, as the summer of 1914 wore on, war clouds continued to grow, and we all began to wonder what lay ahead.

* * *

I had always loved to listen to Granny Mac playing her piano, and especially so that summer. It seemed that I appreciated everything to a greater degree, for some reason. My grandmother could quite well have become a famous concert pianist. Her fingers travelled over the piano keys as though they were a part of the piano, and the music emanating was a joy to everyone.

She had given me lessons on her piano, just as she had taught many of the Caldwells, but I was not as talented in that direction as I might have been. Little Cal, on the other hand, soon began to show definite signs of interest in learning more, and Granny Mac was delighted.

"Finally, one member of the family will enjoy playing the piano as I have done," she proclaimed one day. "Sarah, I'm convinced your youngest son will be a great pianist one day."

Cal looked up at his grandmother and his mother and merely smiled. Then he opened his big brown eyes widely and said, "But I want to fly up in the sky, Granny." It was just before his fourth birthday.

"An airplane pilot!" replied Granny Mac in horror. "Oh Sarah, you must discourage that. Those men are quite mad. The risks they take. It is beyond all imagination!"

"I'm sure Cal will be whatever he wants to be, Mother," she replied. "He is very strong-willed, and I do not intend to break his will."

There often seemed to be tension between my mother and my grandmother, and they frequently disagreed on matters of importance, but the one thing they both agreed adamantly upon concerned the war which, by the summer of 1914, seemed a foregone conclusion. They both agreed that they did not want me to volunteer.

"In any event, Stephen, you are only seventeen. You could not join up until you are eighteen, and by then the war will be over ... if it ever starts."

Granny nodded. "Listen to your mother, Stephen. It is foolish to volunteer."

My father remained silent on the matter. As a man, he understood my feelings. He knew that one had to defend one's country. Although we lived so far from the European stage where events were taking place, we all felt a close bond with, and fierce patriotism for, the old country.

As events unfolded, my future was in limbo. I had finished school and would, in the normal course of events, be heading for university in England or in eastern Canada in September.

Letty had already begun her nursing training at the Royal Jubilee Hospital in Victoria, and she told her parents that once she graduated she also wanted to go to Europe and join the Royal Canadian Army Medical Corps to help the war cause. They were astounded and very concerned, and I think they blamed me because I had said I would be going to England and Letty wanted to be near me. Nonetheless, we went ahead with our plans and made a solemn promise to each other in June, upon hearing the news that the Archduke Ferdinand had been assassinated and war was now imminent.

We sat in the garden of Hamilton House holding hands. "Let's vow to always be together, Letty," I said, and she nodded her head.

"Always, Stephen."

On the 4th August, Great Britain did in fact declare war on Germany, in response to Germany's declaration of war against Russia and France. The unthinkable had happened, and the Canadian government began immediately to ask for volunteers to join a Canadian Expeditionary Force. At that time, Canada had only just over 3,000 regular soldiers, and despite having just turned seventeen, I was one of the first to walk into the recruiting office on Government Street in Victoria and become a volunteer in mid-September.

I handed my birth certificate to the man at the desk. I had altered it to read 1896 instead of 1897, and no one questioned it. After a brief medical examination, I signed my name on the dotted line to volunteer my services for my country.

With youthful patriotism running high, I then prepared myself to face Letty and my family with the news of what I had done.

Letty was the only one who fully understood why I had felt compelled to join up, and she vowed she would also come to England as soon as she was able.

"I may then be sent to France or wherever the battles are being fought, and I will be nearer to you, Stephen."

"Are you sure that is what you want to do? I would much rather you stay safely here while you wait for me to return, Letty. Then we will be married."

She smiled her gentle smile. "Married? Oh? And was that supposed to be a proposal, Mr. Hamilton? If so, it was pretty pitiful."

I blushed as I took her hand. "You know you have always been the only girl for me, Letty, and I love you dearly."

"Knowing and being told are two different things, Mr. Hamilton." She grinned as she poked me in the stomach. "A girl likes to be told she is loved and then formally asked if she will marry the gentleman in question, you know."

"Then consider this my formal proposal, Miss Letitia Caldwell. Will you marry me?"

She giggled. "Well, Mr. Stephen Hamilton, I will give your proposal my most serious consideration and maybe, just maybe, I—"

I pulled her to me and kissed her passionately. "Don't tease me, Letty," I said as we broke apart, both a little startled by the feelings our kiss had stirred. "Just tell me you love me and one day we will be married."

She nodded solemnly. "Yes, Steve, I love you and yes, one day we *will* be married."

"Then we are now officially engaged, and you can wear this ring," I replied, pulling out a small box from my pocket. "I hope you like it."

"Ooooh, Steve, it's beautiful," she replied, and then she began to cry, and soon we were kissing again and then both of us were crying as we clung to one another. It was the most romantic of moments, as we pledged our lives and our hearts to each other for eternity.

Convincing my parents and my grandmother that I had done the right thing by joining the army was quite another thing. My engagement to Letty they could accept, even though they all agreed we were far too young. Only Uncle Teddy sided with us on that issue, saying that young love was often the strongest kind and would indeed last for ever.

But my volunteering was quite another matter. My mother was really angry. "Stephen, you are not even of age. Why? Why on earth would you want to rush off and fight and possibly get killed—?"

My father intercepted her. "Now, now, sweetheart, Stephen is a grown man and he has made the decision he feels he must. I am sure he will be quite safe. He will probably just stay in England in training, and by the time his training is completed, the war will be over."

"Let's pray that is the case," added Granny Mac. "It's such a senseless war ... like all wars. Only the young suffer, because they are used as cannon fodder in the arguments of nations and pompous leaders."

My mother refused to be comforted by my father's words, and Granny Mac's words merely incited her to further fury. Nonetheless, the following Saturday morning I left my desolate family in Victoria and travelled with the first Canadian Expeditionary Force to Vancouver, where we boarded the train for Montreal. On October 3rd I was among the first contingent to sail for England and the glory of war.

In my wallet, I carried a photograph of Letty, and in my heart I held the memory and the scent of her and our last kiss. I knew we would meet again, just as she did. Neither of us feared death, because we were simply doing what had to be done. We were young and in love, and so we believed we were invincible.

Why could my mother not have seen that?

CHAPTER 4

My training on Salisbury Plain in England was a complete and utter farce. Not one of us was a qualified soldier to begin with, and by the end of six weeks, we had made little progress.

Our instructor was a middle-aged army sergeant called Alfred Brinkers, a name that soon got altered by us to *Bonkers*. He knew very little about tactical manoeuvres or warfare of any kind, for he had spent all of us military career in comfortable positions in England, but he did at least insist on keeping us reasonably fit for whatever might befall us in the coming months. This meant making us rise at the ungodly hour of five every morning and then run across country for two miles in our underwear. This was certainly not pleasant in the frosty mornings of October and November in the English countryside, but whenever we objected, he screeched at us in his high-pitched cockney accent:

"You're all a bunch of lily-livered idiots, and if the Germans landed tomorrow they would wipe out each and every one of you," he yelled. I agreed with him.

Our ages ranged from seventeen to twenty-two, and we were not very much qualified at anything in particular. Some had come from the prairie lands of Canada, some from the newspaper business, some from wealthy families who had hoped to train to be lawyers or businessmen, and some had interrupted their university studies to be a part of the so-called glory of war. Many were just plain, ordinary working men, and those were the ones I got along with best.

The Canadian contingent was mixed with the English, but certainly none of us would be an adequate match for the professional killers we were told made up the German army. Not by any stretch of the imagination were we being trained for trench warfare, which was where we were headed.

During the sixth week of this wretched training episode, I received a letter from Letty that raised my spirits. She had written it aboard ship on her way to England, and it was postmarked Liverpool upon her arrival. I knew she was making her way south to join me in Salisbury, where other Red Cross nurses were setting up training camps nearby before heading to Europe. I longed to see her again and share this misery, but first I endured some incredible teasing. Most of the fellows had assumed I wasn't interested in girls, because I had always refused to join them on their beer-soaked evenings seeking female companionship.

The English chaps teased me unmercifully. "Well, well, and we thought the Canuck was a fag," one of them said. "Now, lookee here, he's got a letter from a lady, and it smells of perfume and all."

I blushed. "I told you fellows all along that I had a girl back home. She's all I want, and now she's in England and she'll be here soon. You'd better mind your manners, chaps, because she's a real lady, and we're going to be married after the war."

"Oooh ... listen to this, chaps, the Canuck has got himself a *real* lady! La-de-da-de-da ..."

I let them continue, because suddenly their jokes didn't bother me one bit. I remembered the letter I had written to my parents the night before Letty's arrived that morning. I decided I would add a postscript now, because the first part of it had been rather depressing and might upset them:

Dear Mama and Papa:
December 3rd, 1914
Just a few more lines to let you know that I am still going along in the same old way, one leg at a time. I have recovered from my home sickness now and am trying to concentrate on the task ahead, but our training has been grim and certainly not the kind to give one confidence in the abilities of the British and Canadian Armies. One friend I had made in training camp,

named Bill, had arrived here before me and he has now been transferred to a place called Wareham in Dorsetshire. From there, goodness knows where … we all just have to 'wait and see.'

Maybe you were right in saying that I should at least have gone in for officers' training, but I wanted to be up front and one of the fighting men. I still do.

The chaps in our barracks continue to laugh at me because I won't go out with them looking for girls, but I soon shut them up simply by giving them one of my famous dreaded stares and they practically shiver under my glance! They all think I look young and silly, but I soon will show them that I'm not. In any event, I informed them that I had a girl back home and she was all I wanted.

It was bitterly cold this morning when washing … maybe I'll decide to keep the dirt on in future and use it as an extra overcoat!

Give my regards to all the Caldwells and fondest love to the uncles and Granny Mac.

Ta ta for now (as the Brits say),

Your loving son, Stephen.

P.S. Wonderful news! Just heard from Letty who has arrived safely in Liverpool and is on her way down to the Red Cross Nurses Camp near here. I should see her tomorrow and I can't wait!!!! It looks like we will be together for Christmas—unless we are posted somewhere before that, which I doubt. Now the other chaps are all envious!"

She was even more beautiful than I remembered. We had been apart for only a matter of weeks, but it seemed like a lifetime, and we fell into each other's arms, unable to speak or express our true feelings. Just gazing into her eyes, seeing her smile and touching her beautiful face again made the past weeks of training all a little more bearable.

* * *

Our training continued, and we were told it would probably be February at least before we were moved to France. This suited Letty and me, because we spent every conceivable moment that we could together. On our days off, if they happened to coincide, we took long walks in the brisk December air. Sometimes we went back to her digs, which she shared with a young English girl from Lancashire called Sally. Sally was very diplomatic and always managed to make herself scarce whenever we were there.

On Christmas Eve, Letty and I were off-duty and, with a number of others, had gravitated to the local pub, the Flying Swan. We all drank a little too much and sang all the popular patriotic and romantic songs, with some Christmas carols thrown in for good measure, before dispersing at midnight. I walked Letty home and, much to our delight, Sally was not yet home.

"I think I need a cup of coffee or something to sober me up a bit, Letty," I said.

"Oh, Steve, you're fine. You're just more relaxed now. Come on, let's sit down on the couch. Kiss me, Steve, and wish me a happy Christmas."

I did not need asking twice. Our feelings had grown even stronger since she'd arrived in Salisbury, and it was becoming more and more difficult to restrain them. Living in that somewhat surreal world, so far from everything familiar, it was easy to forget the values and traditions we had grown up with. I still loved and respected Letty desperately, and had we been back in Victoria, I would no more have seduced her that night than fly to the moon.

I would definitely have thought about it, of course, because I was, after all, a man, but one just did not do "it" with the girl you were going to marry one day. The girl you considered pure and above reproach. There were other women around who would, for a price, willingly cater to a man's frustrations. Not that I had ever used one. At seventeen, I was still as virginal as Letty.

But on that night, Letty was just as desperate as I was, and soon we were undressing and touching each other in places that we knew were forbidden. But somehow it all seemed right. War was all around us, and we both knew that soon we would be in the thick of it.

"I want to know how it feels to be really loved by you, Steve," she whispered. "I want you to make love to me and make me a woman tonight, in case ..."

She never finished her sentence. I wouldn't allow her to, because I was already far too excited. In my inexperience, I probably hurt her, but she didn't complain. She simply smiled at me after it was over and said, "Now, whatever happens, Stephen, I will always have this night to remember. I truly feel like your wife now." And then, with a twinkle in her eye, she added, "I may even have conceived a baby tonight. We didn't use any protection."

"Oh God, Letty. I hope not—not right now, with all that's happening. We're so young—and supposing I'm killed? What would happen to you? What then?"

"Oh, Stephen Hamilton, stop that talk. You will *not* be killed. And, if we do have a baby, we will manage. What is meant to be is meant to be."

She was such a fatalist, and I adored her. We kissed again and then made love again, this time more slowly and with a little more expertise. All too soon, there came a light tap on the door, and Sally was home. She diplomatically allowed us time to dress before entering and wishing us both a happy Christmas. I didn't doubt that she'd been spending an evening of passion with her own fellow, so she understood only too well.

Letty and I had three more opportunities to make love following that Christmas Eve. And then, early in February of 1915, word came that our contingent would be moved to France. I bade a tearful farewell to my beloved girl before we sailed across the English Channel. Letty also knew by then that her group of nurses would soon be transferred to the field, so somehow we felt convinced our paths would cross again soon.

I continued to write long letters home to my grandmother and to my parents, and they in turn wrote back to me. Many of those letters caught up to me before we left England. One in particular from my mother warmed my heart and made my volunteering to fight in this beastly war worthwhile. We had parted company in Victoria in such a painful manner, but her letter now made me feel at peace that she had finally accepted my decision.

My dearest Stephen:

Your father and I still miss you terribly but your long, newsy letters are a great comfort to us. We treasure each and every one, and, because your beautiful prose is so descriptive, we feel we were there with you through that beastly training in such unpleasant conditions.

Most people realize now that the war will continue for a while, and we pray for your safety if and when you are sent to the battle field. We pray for Letty also, and all those brave women like her that are nursing our sons and husbands in that foreign land.

It is quite unbelievable how civilized people can be so stupid ... this is not a criticism of you, dear. After you left, I thought a great deal about what you said concerning conscience and doing the right thing, and you are absolutely right. I suppose I taught you too well as a child that one must think of others and step in to help where we can. This is basically the same thing. We cannot allow these tyrants to take over and destroy our peaceful world. We must help England, our mother country, and I, like many other mothers around the world, must temporarily sacrifice my son to this noble cause.

So, Stephen, you were right! You see, your mother has finally managed to admit it, and to say, I am immeasurably proud of you.

That is not to say, however, that I don't still wish you were safely here at home. You are still my beloved son and always will be ... but now, at least, I can truthfully say that I understand your strong motivation.

Her letter made me smile, and it warmed my heart on the coldest nights of fear and despair that lay ahead.

In our particular division was a brigade surgeon called John McCrae who also wrote the most beautiful poetry. I was immediately drawn to him because of his sensitivity, and we enjoyed some long talks together. Whereas my own creative muse had been silent for some months, he seemed even more inspired by the terrible sights of war as the months progressed.

And terrible sights they were. We saw our first fighting of the Great War in March of 1915 at a place called *Neuve Chapell*, and by the middle of April the First Canadian Division, of which I was a part, took over a section of the French trenches near Ypres in Belgium. And there, our innocence and inexperience was put to the test as we witnessed some of the heaviest and bloodiest fighting of all.

* * *

There are no words to describe the sights and sounds I saw over the days that followed.

On the 17th April we were moved to the front lines. The weather was wet and gloomy, and for most of the time we were practically waist-high in mud. We were convinced things could not possibly get any worse, but we were wrong.

To our left were the 45th division of French soldiers, and to the right two British divisions, so we initially felt reasonably safe. But, on the 22nd of April, the German troops, who were quite obviously far more experienced than we at this, unleashed their deadliest weapon—chlorine gas.

The gas was hurled at us with mortars, and we were totally unprepared. Large green and yellow clouds hung in clusters, mingling with the damp fog before dropping into the trenches and making the men in them choke. Some died instantly. As the rest of us scrambled desperately to escape this horror with wet pieces of cloth covering our mouths, many soldiers were literally incinerated by the gas, which burned their skin. I heard some gasping for breath as their lungs melted.

I coughed and choked as I scrambled out of my trench, barely aware of the chaos around me. We survivors dragged ourselves in retreat, barely able to see or breathe, holding each other up as best we could. I'd had barely enough time to soak my rag in muddy water; others were soaking their rags in their own urine. Miraculously we came across reinforcements from the rear who were handing out goggles to those who had come through the initial attack. We put on these amateur gas masks, which managed to filter out some of the poison in the air before it entered our mouths and eyes. But the gas continued to come, along with shells being fired at regular intervals.

I was holding on to one fellow, each of us trying to encourage the other as we stumbled along. I didn't recognize him as part of our unit, but I kept pulling him with me and talking. Then I realized that I was doing all the talking and he was no longer responding. The rag had fallen from his face, which had now turned purple in that freakish light. Or was it the colour of blood now spurting from his mouth, I wondered. He slipped from my grasp to the ground. I realized in despair that I was too weak to help him further. In that moment, I asked myself where the glory was in such an ignoble and undignified death. I don't remember much after that. I think I lost consciousness.

I just know that when I next opened my eyes, I was gazing into the face of Letty. I thought for a moment I had died and gone to Heaven. It seemed the only possible explanation.

CHAPTER 5

LETTY

The first battle of Ypres was fought between the end of October and the 17th of November of 1914, while Stephen had still been in training in England and I had been working at a nursing station nearby.

That first battle had been fought with cavalry and foot battalions firing shells and other heavy artillery. The British, with French reinforcements, had managed to hold on for weeks and were finally relieved from the trenches shortly before the high winds and blizzards of winter put a temporary halt to the hostilities.

But a second battle at Ypres this year had gone completely differently when the Germans introduced gas into their warfare. Defeat was obvious, but the bravery of the men coming into our station was beyond belief.

At the beginning of May, one division was officially removed from the front line, after suffering more than 1,000 fatalities. I prayed every day that Stephen would be among the other 3,058 casualties who were sent to nearby Red Cross camps or nursing stations like ours.

I had been working at a makeshift hospital camp just outside Flanders for three weeks, and, having heard of the catastrophe on the front line, where I knew Stephen had been posted, I'd spent every possible moment frantically searching for him, as man upon injured man was brought into the camp.

When he finally arrived on a stretcher, he was unconscious and near to death, but I wept for joy that he was at least alive. Perhaps I could still nurse him back to health. For the next three days I stayed by his side, wiping his brow and willing him to open his eyes.

When the doctor ordered me to work on other patients, I refused. "He's my fiancé," I kept saying. "I can't leave him." Eventually he and the other nurses gave up urging me to do my duty. They all understood the pain I was experiencing, seeing my beloved like this.

Then, one morning, Steve regained consciousness and opened his sore, bloodshot eyes.

"Letty? Is that you?" he whispered. "Where am I? Am I dreaming?"

"Yes, it's me, dearest, and you're not dreaming. You're safe now. You are going to be all right."

"What happened?"

"The gas ... it was horrid."

"Ghastly ... did many die?'

I nodded.

"But I have no memory of any of that or how I got here. Did a stretcher bearer find me?"

"Yes, my darling. You were brought in three days ago."

"So I was one of the lucky ones?"

I nodded again. "Your lungs are a little damaged—enough, I hope, to allow you to be sent home."

"Home? No, Letty. I must get better and go back ... there are so many of my friends there. I cannot leave them."

I patted his hand and smiled. "We'll see, Steve. We'll see what the doctor says when he comes back."

But when Doctor Blake returned an hour later, he pronounced Stephen fit to return to the front.

"But he's still sick," I screamed. "I want to talk to someone else in authority. He should be sent back to England to recover in a proper hospital."

"Oh, is that so, Nurse Caldwell? And what makes you an expert?"

"Common sense, sir."

"So, what do you think would happen if I sent all our patients back to England to recover? There would be no one left to fight, and the Germans would overrun us in no time flat."

I had been firmly put in my place. But I refused to give up. Stephen was still very sick. He had a hacking cough, and his skin was yellowish.

"Doctor Blake, I want to talk to one of the surgeons, or someone who can see that my fiancé is not fit to fight right now. Please ..."

"Nurse Caldwell, please stop the theatrics. I have no time for this. Private Hamilton will be returning to the front tomorrow."

"This is madness, sir," I said again. "None of these men here are fit for warfare. It makes no sense."

He could see my desperation, but he merely shrugged in frustration. "I wish I could send them all back home to recover, Nurse Caldwell, I really do, but our orders are to allow them to rest for a while until their wounds heal. Then they must return to their units. There is nothing else I can do. This is war. " He turned and walked away

War? War? Bloody war? Where is the glory in this? I hate war!

I didn't speak my thoughts aloud to Stephen, because he agreed with the doctor.

"Letty, the doctor is right. But you must believe in us. We will come through this. I know we will. One day we will be together again back in Victoria."

"Oh, Stephen. I can't bear seeing you go back to the front again. How can they possibly think you are fit enough to fight? It's ridiculous," I cried. "I thought it was a miracle seeing you alive this time. Can I expect God to give us another miracle?"

"Letty, hold on, my love," he said, but I kept sobbing.

"I'm not even pregnant, Steve. I so wanted your baby."

"You will have my child one day, I promise," he said, with youthful optimism. Despite all the horrors he must already have seen, he still believed in our own invincibility.

I so wish I did.

CHAPTER 6

STEPHEN

I can still see her weeping on the morning I left to continue our pathetic assault against the Germans. She wiped away her tears as she kissed me and gave me one final hug. Her bravery inspired me to also be strong. I had been allowed just one more day of grace at the camp, and then three of us in our unit were sent back into the fray.

We soon realized we were fighting a losing battle, but I kept asking myself what would happen if we had all decided to give up. We had to go on and keep fighting. There was now no other choice. Word had already reached our unit that the Germans were becoming more wary of the Canadian forces and were beginning to respect and even fear our tenacity. The tide was slowly but surely turning, and I wanted to be a part of the offensive that would annihilate this demonic enemy and bring peace to our world once again.

But during the next weeks and months of unspeakable horror, before we finally reached the Somme in August of 1916 to begin another major offensive against Germany, I was more and more aware of how futile and ugly this war had become. There was little glory left as we struggled on, buoyed up by the dubious knowledge that finally the Germans were beginning to fear the Allied troops and were even treating the Canadian forces with more respect.

I was promoted to corporal and led our unit on assaults into one battle after another. Horrors became commonplace, everyday occurrences, and unimaginable slaughter became mundane. Nonetheless, I still felt proud to contribute to the peace I was sure would come, eventually.

* * *

Our division took over the front lines near the village of Courcelette. I still felt weak and coughed frequently, never having really shaken the effects of that deadly gas at Ypres.

For months, we had lived in filth and misery, hacking out crude dugouts in the trenches as we slowly advanced. There in those dugouts, we would sit and smoke, which truthfully only made us cough more, but at least it gave us some comfort. Illness ran rampant in our division, and infestations of fleas and lice led to trench fever, from which we all suffered. In addition, a steady diet of nothing more than corned beef, biscuits and overly sweet tea made many of us prone to boils and other skin problems. It was hell on earth.

Before our division even reached Courcelette, we suffered a heavy loss of life. Bodies had been left to rot in the trenches because there simply were not enough stretcher bearers to take them away. The stench was unbearable. Medics were kept fully occupied trying to assist those who were still alive. They could do little about those who were already gone.

The major attack began on September 15, 1916. We were assisted now by armoured tanks, which had been recently introduced into the war, nicknamed "the engines of war." These powerful beasts enabled us to move forward more quickly and finally take Courcelette.

The chill of an early winter was already in the air, but we still worked mainly waist-high in mud and water. The shelling continued until our heads hurt so badly from the cacophony of war that we wanted to scream. But we fought on, taking one trench after another, our ultimate aim being to join the rest of the allied forces at Vimy Ridge.

I remember one night in particular and the conversation I had with a chap called Barney who was beside me in the trench. He had grown up on a farm in Alberta, and we exchanged stories of our youth. *Youth?* I remember thinking that was a joke. Had I ever been young?

I simply couldn't remember. My eyes had seen sights that no man should ever see. My youthful innocence had long since been destroyed.

There was an eerie silence that night that, in itself, was unusual. Barney and I kept whispering back and forth, trying to dispel the feeling of dread we both had.

"What could this silence mean? Are the Germans planning some other gruesome torture?" Barney said.

I still had nightmares about the gas at Ypres. Could they be planning something equally deadly?

Before I could reply, the shelling began again. But now it was coming from every direction. I turned toward Barney as I automatically raised my own rifle in a gesture of defence. His body was still there; oh yes, it was definitely still there beside me. I could swear his heart was beating beneath his bloodstained uniform.

But his head ... dear God Almighty! His head had been blown to smithereens. Only his unseeing eyes were still peering up at me from some other place, seemingly asking what had just happened. Where am I?

But I had no answers. No answers for Barney. No answers for me or for any of the thousands of other fools who had enthusiastically joined this madness called war which, in our ignorance, we had once glorified and exalted.

I realized in that moment that I would probably soon join Barney, so I prayed it would happen quickly and without too much pain. I thought of Letty and remembered our love, which I hoped would transcend this life and carry on to the next. And I thought of home and of my parents and all the good things that still existed in this world, even though the battle fields of Europe had become completely insane. I dreamed of being home again at Hamilton House. I wanted to play with young Cal. I wanted to visit Providence and hear Granny Mac playing her piano. I wanted to see the snow-capped Olympic mountains and smell green grass and beautiful flowers. I wanted to be—alive again.

Then I saw two of my men, Austin and Charles, running toward the open fire. A shell exploded, and in the brilliance of its flare, I saw their bodies fly into the air and land a few yards ahead. Without thinking, I ran to them and began to drag them back to our trench. They were my men, but I didn't know if they were dead or alive. It just made sense to do something.

But, in that moment I also knew with certainty that I would never reach Vimy Ridge.

CHAPTER 7

LETTY

I staggered from the main nursing tent into the small area alongside, where we took our breaks. As I sank wearily into a chair, I noticed a rat in the corner.

"Stop staring at me," I yelled at it, but it didn't move. It knew I had no strength left to even shoo it away.

I had been on my feet for the past twelve hours and could no longer keep my head up. I rested it on my arms on the hard table and tried to make sense of the madness all around me. I had arrived with two other nurses at this clearing station three weeks ago, but we soon all learned there was little we or anyone else could do for the men who were brought in on stretchers. Other than giving them morphine and making them more comfortable, it seemed to be a lost cause. And now, even our morphine supply was running low.

This station was practically inside the trenches; we were on ground recently evacuated by the Germans. Because we were so close to the action, we heard shell fire on three sides of us all day, and the noise was deafening. The station consisted of two tents holding about seventy patients each, and as they were lying on stretchers so close together, even bandaging them was nigh on impossible. Another small adjoining tent was where we slept.

Today, like Doctor Blake and the other eight nurses, I had been caring for one patient after another as they were carried in on blood-stained stretchers from the battlefield. My back was so sore from bending over them, I felt sure that if I sat too long I would never be able to stand up again.

As I rested my head on my folded arms on the table, trying to turn off my brain for at least this five-minute break, I was barely aware of the blood that smeared my blue skirt and blouse. But my stiff white collar was choking me, so I pulled at it.

"Nurse ... Nurse Caldwell," a nearby voice called my name. Doctor Blake was standing there with Milly, one of the other nurses. Why were they calling me so soon? I had barely sat down. Surely it wasn't time to go back to work yet. But Milly was walking toward me and placing a gentle hand on my shoulder. "Letty," she whispered. "There is news of Stephen, dear." By now, they all knew that I'd been waiting for news of him for months.

I jumped up, immediately alert. "Is he here? Has he been brought in?"

She shook her head.

Doctor Blake spoke then, but his words made no sense. "Your fiancé's name has appeared on the deceased list, which just came in, Letty. Corporal Stephen Hamilton. I'm so very sorry. The list was updated yesterday." Doctor Howard never called the nurses by our first names. He was always so formal. Why was he calling me *Letty* now? Did he feel remorse because he had sent Stephen back to fight?

"No—no, that cannot be ... it must be a mistake," I said. "Please tell me it's a mistake."

"Sit down, Letty dear," Milly said. "Here, drink some water."

I pushed away the cup she offered, and water splashed everywhere. The world was spinning. Between exhaustion and horror, I couldn't think straight. All I knew was that Stephen couldn't be dead. He said he would return. We would have a life together. We would be married and have children.

"Let me see the list," I screamed.

Doctor Blake handed it to me. "You're off duty now, Letty. You're in shock, so I want you to go to your quarters and lie down."

I read down the list until I came to the names beginning with "H"—and there it was, just as he said. Corporal Stephen Hamilton, killed in action.

"NO! NO! Not Stephen ..."

They tried to steer me out of the tent, but I rebelled. "I'm not leaving. I must work. Please let me work. I need to work ..."

I could barely stand, but once I took one step I began to feel stronger. I knew I couldn't stop now. I had to keep going until this made some sense. I had to take care of these other poor men. All of them belonged to someone—a mother, a father, a husband, a lover—just as Stephen had. And now I must try and save them all.

Hours later, the stretcher bearers stopped coming in with more bodies. It was night by then. The noise had stopped, and an eerie silence fell over the air. No more shells. No more firing. Just silence—which somehow seemed worse than all the horrific familiar noises.

As we nurses stumbled out of the work station and back to our sleeping quarters to try to catch a few hours of sleep before it would all begin over again, I heard Milly's voice and wasn't sure if she was talking to me or to herself.

"Where is the glory in this bloody war?"

I shook my head, too weary to even reply. That's when I noticed another rat lurking in a corner. Without thinking, I ran at it and kicked it before it had time to scamper away. Then I kept on kicking and stomping on it until it was dead. I took great satisfaction in seeing its blood spurt everywhere and completely cover my boots.

I had at least killed one of the many evils of this damnable war—and it felt damn good.

* * *

Two days later, I found a few moments to write a letter to my parents, assuring them I was still safe in France and had decided to stay on in Europe to help me heal from losing Stephen. I tried to explain that I needed time to help others, because I had not been able to help Stephen—but how could they possibly understand when I didn't understand it myself?

I then wrote a second letter of condolence to Stephen's parents, assuring them that Stephen had been very brave at the end and had given his life for his country. But was he brave, I wondered. More than likely he was sickened by it all and very scared, just like me.

Lastly I wrote to dear Granny Mac at Providence. But none of those letters really explained how bitter I was really feeling. What I really wanted to tell them all could never be said.

How could I possibly describe the sights I had seen and how much I despised this war and how I hated what it had made me become and what it had done to us all? I also knew my letters would not arrive before they would all have been notified of Stephen's death, anyway—so what was the point of writing at all? But still, I did, and then placed the letters in the mail bag for pick-up. Meanwhile, I managed to bury my own grief by working hard, day in and day out. It was Nurse Edith Cavell who had first inspired me to work on the front lines, and it was her courage that now inspired me to keep going throughout the coming year.

On top of all the other miseries, it seemed to rain non-stop during the winter of 1916 and well into the spring of 1917. Our tents were always leaking, and our oil stoves threw out little heat. But eventually I became immune to the cold, the sickness, the blood, the missing limbs and the limbs we had to amputate under deplorably unhygienic conditions. I tried to ignore the infestation of rats and fleas and all the infections we couldn't cure. All we could do for the men was to provide comfort in their last agonizing hours on earth. But it was never enough.

* * *

Then one day, in early March of 2017, a young lad in incredible pain crawled into our clearing station on all fours. He was not brought in on a stretcher, even though he was in very bad shape—and that in itself was unusual. He collapsed on the ground, and two of us carried him to a cot that had just been vacated. His fever was raging and his eyes glassy.

"Help me ... please help me!" he screamed. I tried to assess his injuries as he tossed and turned and kept screaming.

"The pain ... I can't bear the pain any longer." His right foot and two of his fingers on his right hand were missing. We gave him aspirin for the fever.

"What's your name, sweetheart?" I asked as I tried to locate his identification tag.

"Joe ... I ran away. I couldn't stand it anymore. I'm a coward ..."

"That's okay, Joe," I said. "You're safe now ..." But I knew he wasn't. He must be a deserter as well as being near death.

"Are you both the angels of mercy? Where am I? Is this heaven?"

I smiled at him. "No Joe, we're just nurses. I'm Letty and this is Milly, and you are at a clearing station, where we will help you as best we can. But I'm afraid we're not angels."

"Angels ..." he repeated.

I called Doctor Blake over, and he agreed that all we could do was to continue to make Joe comfortable. He now had another young doctor assisting him, but they both looked grim as they examined Joe further.

"We'll put you on the next ambulance, Joe. When it arrives, you will be taken to the nearest field hospital, where they can do more for you than we can here," Doctor Blake said. He didn't mention that it would probably be a long time before the next ambulance arrived. Joe continued to scream in pain.

Milly then left to attend to another patient, and in a split second, Joe's left hand came towards me, pushing me so hard that I fell backwards onto the floor. It happened so quickly that I didn't have time to see the revolver that must still have been in his belt. All I knew was that a deafening shot rang through the air and pieces of Joe's face were flying in the air.

The two doctors ran over to me, lifted me to my feet and then examined Joe, who had placed the gun inside his mouth in an attempt to end his agony.

"God Almighty, he shot himself in the head," Dr. Blake said. "The bullet has taken out his eye, but it's lodged in his skull somewhere. If there's an ambulance in the area, get it here immediately. Now!" he yelled at us all. "This man will need surgery on his face. Maybe he can still be saved with the right operating tools ..."

His voice dwindled off. Saved? Why? Why would we want to save this poor young man? He had wanted to die when he first came in. He couldn't stand the unbearable pain. He had run away from his unit, and then, when things became even more horrendous, he had tried to shoot himself. So why would we want to save him? Why were we trained to save lives of those who didn't want to be saved?

So we were the angels of mercy? But where was the mercy, when we all knew that even if they saved Joe's life and repaired his wounds in hospital, he would probably be tried for treason for being a deserter. I failed to see any mercy in that.

The next ambulance came within an hour, and Joe was taken away. Dr. Blake came over to me and put his arm around my shoulder. "I'm so sorry, Letty—for everything. So very, very sorry."

"Me, too," I replied as I fell into his comforting embrace. "Me, too ..."

A week later, we heard that Joe had died on the operating table and, despite my oath to save lives, on that one particular night in this living hell on earth, I thanked God for Joe's merciful death.

CHAPTER 8

SARAH (Victoria, BC, October 1916)

Winter was settling in early that year. We all recalled the previous one, when Victoria had been deluged with snow and many outlying areas were isolated for weeks.

We hoped this coming winter would not be a repeat. But how could we complain when so many of our beloved sons, brothers and husbands were suffering so terribly on the battle fields of Europe? We'd last heard from Stephen in May, at which time he was safe in a Red Cross camp in Belgium. Letty, who was nursing him, had helped him write the letter.

Our next news came from Letty herself, who told us that Stephen had recovered from the effects of the gas at that terrible battle at Ypres but had now been sent back into the fray. She had word that his division was holding on as they continued their offensive, taking town upon town. The allies were aiming eventually to meet at Vimy Ridge. During all those many months, we waited patiently for a letter from Stephen himself, but nothing came. I had continued to write to him, hoping somehow the letters would reach him.

Throughout the long summer of 1916 and now well into October, we patiently waited for more news, never knowing from day to day where Stephen was or if he was safe. My nerves were wracked with worry, and I did a great deal of praying.

"What were you thinking about, dearest?" Ernest asked me suddenly as he, Caleb and I, sat in the drawing room on one cool October afternoon. Ernest was working from home that day instead of going into the office, and at four o'clock we were all having tea together.

Cal was now six years old and a very active little boy. Although he had come to us late in life, after many years of trying to conceive another child and Ernest blaming himself for our failures, we had finally been blessed with another son. To please my mother, I had named him Caleb. She took my attempt to honour her own long-lost little son stoically and with little emotion. I thought she would have been delighted, but then, my mother had never been able to show joy at anything I did. Since her displeasure upon discovering my one marital indiscretion with Willow a few years ago, I felt she always regarded me with even more distaste than before.

I suppose *distaste* is a harsh word. Maybe I misjudged her. Nonetheless, I sensed that I never completely measured up to her high expectations of me. Our son Cal, however, had become the joy of our life, and I knew that my mother also held a special place in her heart for him. Not that she ever favoured him over Stephen. I will give her that. She never held Stephen's accident of birth against him, or against me. I was sure she loved both her grandsons equally.

On that particular October afternoon, Cal was, for once, quiet and fully occupied with cutting out pictures of air machines and sticking them in his scrapbook. The fire had been made up, and it was cosy sitting there all together, basking in its warmth. If only this black cloud was not hanging over us about Stephen. If only we knew he was safe. Not knowing was the worst part.

I tried to sound casual and bright as I answered Ernest's question. "I was just hoping we might get a letter from Stephen this week. It's been so long. And even when we do receive one, it arrives weeks after he has written it."

"Well, remember that Joe and Emily had one from Letty last week and there was no bad news, so let's keep thinking positively, dearest. He may even be on his way home for some leave."

"Oh, Ernest, how I wish that were the case. And I admire Letty so much. She is so brave to be in the midst of it all, nursing those poor boys. But she wrote that letter back in August. Anything could have happened since then."

Cal looked up. "Is Steve going to be home soon, Mumsy?" he asked. I smiled at him. I wondered where on earth he had come up with that ridiculous name for me. Cal always liked to be different. To him, I was Mumsy and Ernest was Pops.

"We hope so, Cal. We certainly hope so," I told him.

"Good, then he can tell me all about the air machines they are using in the war."

"Well, he is in the infantry, son," said Ernest. "I doubt he sees much air warfare."

"He must have seen some air machines though, Pops. Gosh, I envy him."

"Oh Cal, war is such a terrible thing. Don't envy poor Stephen. Your brother is defending our country and being terribly brave, but war is—" I paused in mid-sentence as Ernest suddenly stood up, placing his teacup on the side table. He was now glancing out of the window.

"What is it, dear?" I asked.

He didn't reply at once, so I turned around and looked out as well, to see the young boy who delivered telegrams riding up our driveway on his bicycle. In his hand was a dreaded yellow telegram.

"Oh my God!" I said.

"It may be from Steve himself, telling us he is coming home on leave," replied Ernest heading for the front door. "Don't think the worst, Sarah."

I dismissed his warning, because I had known for far too long that a telegram being delivered in this day and age usually meant one thing—bad news from the front. I quickly ran after my husband, with Cal close at my heels.

"Cal, run to the kitchen and find Nanny. Please, dear, hurry."

I did not want my little boy there if the news was bad. He looked at me in surprise. "But, Mumsy, suppose—"

"Go, Cal," his father told him more authoritatively, obviously having the same thought. Cal, somewhat mystified, scurried away.

Ernest then opened the front door just as the boy was propping his bicycle against the porch railing. "Two telegrams for Mr. and Mrs. Hamilton," he said.

Ernest took them and gave the boy some money.

"Thank you, sir," the boy replied politely as he turned and went on his way, unaware of what turmoil he might have left behind.

My heart was beating far too quickly as Ernest ripped open the first telegram. I watched his eyes and I knew immediately.

"Ernest!" I grabbed the telegrams from him. "No ... oh dear God, no ..."

My eyes were bleary and the words on the yellow paper were at first distorted, but their meaning was only too clear.

Regret to inform you that your son Corporal Stephen Ernest Hamilton is missing in action.

The second read: *"Corporal Stephen Ernest Hamilton was reported killed on September 27, 1916, while valiantly engaged in battle. The Canadian Expeditionary Forces express their deepest sympathy. Further details will be sent to you by the War Office at a later date.*

My nightmare had come true. Why did I need two pieces of stupid paper to tell me my son was gone? The room was suddenly spinning around me, and I was screaming his name, before sinking into a black space of the deepest despair and grief.

CHAPTER 9

"Take me to Providence, Ernest," I pleaded.

Apparently I had fainted, and my husband had carried me back into the drawing room. I was now lying on the sofa, Ernest holding a damp cloth to my forehead.

Nanny, Cal and our maid, Esther, were standing around me, their faces white. I suppose they had all come running upon hearing the commotion in the hall.

"You are in no state to go anywhere, dearest."

"What's wrong, Mumsy?" asked Cal. "Is it news about Stevie?"

I looked into his handsome little face, and his big brown eyes melted my heart. He had adored his older brother. How could I tell him? I turned my head away in despair, while Ernest took his hand and led him over to the fireplace. I heard him whispering to his son, "We've had some really bad news, Caleb. Your brother has been killed in battle, but he was very brave—"

"He was a hero, right?"

"Oh yes, Cal, he was definitely a hero."

Nanny and Esther were crying uncontrollably, and they were both irritating me violently.

"Ernest," I repeated. "Take me to Providence *now*. I want to see my mother."

"But Sarah ..." He ran his hands through his hair. I knew he was suffering too, but I had to get out of the house immediately, and if he would not take me, I would go alone. I needed the security of Providence. I needed my mother.

I stood up slowly and, although a little wobbly, began to walk toward the door. "I will take the car and drive myself."

"No Sarah!" he shouted at me. "You will not go alone. I will take you. Nanny, please take care of Cal. Go upstairs to the nursery with him and let him play with his toys. We won't be long. There will be many people to notify, but naturally Mrs. Hamilton wants to tell her mother first."

"Yes, sir," replied the sniffling Nanny. I briefly hugged Cal and then headed outside, unmindful of taking a warm coat with me. Ernest followed in silence. There seemed nothing for us to say to each other.

As we drove down the familiar roads leading to Providence, I began to shake uncontrollably. I knew that shock was setting in by then, but I had to keep going. I had to do something to try to obliterate this horror. To try to make it go away so that it would not be true. My mother would know what to do.

Perhaps it was a mistake, I thought. Or did I actually say that aloud to Ernest?

It *must* be a mistake, I thought. It had to be. Everything looked the same at Providence as we drove up the driveway toward the front door, which was opened by Mrs. Stapleton. Nothing had changed there.

"Oh, good afternoon, Mrs. Hamilton," she said as I rushed passed her.

"Where's my mother?"

"She's upstairs in her sitting room, I believe. Good afternoon, Mr. Hamilton."

Ernest nodded. "Mrs. Stapleton, would you please go up and let her know we're here and—"

But I was already racing up the staircase. I turned to see Ernest shrug at an alarmed Mrs. Stapleton, before following me upstairs.

I burst into the master suite and through to mother's sitting room. The fire had been made up and she was sitting beside it, writing in her journal.

"Sarah! My dear, whatever is wrong?" She looked up at me in alarm, always able to detect my mood.

I thrust the now crumpled telegram at her. "He's gone, Mother ... they say Stephen's dead, but it can't be true, can it?"

She stood up quickly to take the telegram from me, and it struck me then how majestic and regal she looked, even though she was so small. Her lips quivered slightly but there was no other immediate emotional reaction.

"Oh dear God," she simply said. "Not our Stephen."

"That's what I said, Mother. It has to be a mistake, doesn't it? Letty said he was fine in her last letter. His division was making such good progress. The war would be over soon, she told us, so ... it simply can't be true."

I began pacing up and down in agitation. Ernest took my arm and forced me to sit down, but I brushed him away. "He's not dead, I tell you. Not Stephen. It must be a mistake."

"Dearest, they would not have sent us a telegram unless—"

"Unless what?" I screamed at him. "Unless his body really was shot to smithereens somewhere on some foreign land? Stop trying to pacify me, Ernest, and stop calling me *dearest*. I can't bear it. This can't be true. I simply won't believe it!"

"But Ernest is right, Sarah. They don't make mistakes about these things."

Ernest started stroking my arm to calm me, but it merely made me more agitated. "Stop it! Stop it! Both of you. Ernest go away. Go ... and talk to Uncle Edward, or to Uncle James, or Joe and Emily. Please go."

"I cannot leave you like this, Sarah. You are so distraught."

"And what in God's name do you expect me to be? They have sent me a stupid telegram telling me my son is dead, and it simply is not true."

"He's my son, too—"

"No! No he's not. So you can't possibly understand." I was screaming at him now, and I was making no sense. In my heart, I knew that Ernest had always been the truest and best of fathers to Stephen.

We had never again referred to Stephen's true origins since the day we were married.

Some part of me wondered how I could possibly have been so cruel and heartless to him by saying what I'd just said, but I continued my senseless tirade. "Get out! Go away. I want to be with my mother now. Only she can truly understand my pain."

He walked slowly to the door, his utter sorrow and despair so apparent. Mother followed him, and they whispered together for a moment.

"She doesn't mean it, Ernest. It's only the grief talking. Believe me. She will need you again soon. Just be patient with her," I heard Mother say before she closed the door and came back to sit with me.

She took both my hands in hers as she faced me, but, more than anything, I wanted her arms around me. I wanted to be her little girl again. This pain was too much to bear.

"Sarah, I am so terribly sorry. Stephen was an angel, a beautiful, sensitive young boy, but he was doing what he wanted to do. None of us could have stopped him. His fate was already laid out for him."

"Fate! Fate! How can it be fate for an innocent boy to die in such a senseless way? You should know what I mean, Mother. My little brother Caleb was only two years old and he died. Why? It makes no sense."

"I agree, Sarah. It makes no sense. But what we have to do is to somehow try to *find* the sense in it. Try to find the reason. I made ... I made so many mistakes myself back then. I turned from your father, and I turned from everyone. Even having you and Bertie and Teddy was never enough for me, it seemed. Please don't make the mistakes I did. You still have Ernest, who loves you so much, and you still have little Cal to think about. Life has to go on. Your papa told me that before he died. He was dying, but he still was able to tell me that life has to go on and we have to find a way to endure."

"But my life is so miserable ... Oh, Mama, first I lost Etienne, then Papa and Bowery, and now Stephen. I did try. I always tried to go on ... but not after this, not after this. Stephen was all I had left of Etienne. Can't you see that?"

She nodded and squeezed my hands in hers, and then she did something I would never have expected: she pulled me into her arms and hugged me tightly to her.

"I can see, Sarah. Believe me, I can see. I should have given you more love to get you through this now. But I had so much to learn about love myself. Loving someone was something I had to learn how to do—when no one had ever showed me how."

We stayed in each other's arms for a long time, she rocking me back and forth as we both cried together for all that might have been.

Finally, we pulled apart and gazed into each other's faces, and actually managed to smile because we both looked so ghastly, our faces pale, drawn and tear-stained.

"Oh, Mama," I said. "I want to be strong like you."

"You will be, my pet," she replied. "You will be."

And then she pulled me to my feet. "We will help one another, Sarah. We will lean on each other for support. We have lost someone very precious to us both, but today you have been the one to give me a gift in return."

"A gift? How?"

"You are so like your papa," she replied. "You have his spirit and determination. Both of you have helped me learn to love and to give love back. And that is an immeasurable gift." Then, hand in hand, we left her room, descended the stairs and faced the world.

I was suddenly glad that Ernest had not left without me after all. He was still sitting in the drawing room with his head in his hands, and he was sobbing quietly.

I ran over to him and knelt down beside him.

"I'm so sorry, Ernest. I was cruel for saying what I did. He *was* every bit your son, and you were a wonderful father to him. Please forgive me."

He pulled me to him, and finally we embraced each other in our deep sorrow. He never questioned my outburst after that, but he must have realized my mother had also known I was pregnant by another man when we were married.

CHAPTER 10

LETTY

I stayed in France for another year after Stephen's death, as the war continued to rage in all its horror. Nothing made sense to me anymore, so I continued to nurse the wounded. There were many days when I wished I could die.

In the summer of 1917, I was posted to a hospital away from the front lines. I felt better there because I was at least able to see progress as men recovered from their wounds and often were sent home—mostly with a missing leg or arm—and I felt myself wishing that had happened to Stephen so that he would at least be away from this abominable war, but still alive.

By then, I had heard from my parents and from Stephen's, and I knew how very badly they had all taken the news of Stephen's death. I felt guilty for staying away from Victoria, but I simply wasn't ready to return just yet. I couldn't face all that was familiar back home without him.

In the spring of 1918, I was sent back to England, to a field hospital for recovering war veterans just outside London, but two days after my arrival I went down with a miserable cold that soon turned into a bad case of influenza.

I was placed in isolation because my fever was so high, but I was in and out of consciousness for a few days so I don't recall much—just unfamiliar faces appearing and disappearing again in front of me.

"Where am I?" I remember asking in one of my more lucid moments. The face looking down at me appeared to be a nurse.

"Ah, Nurse Caldwell, you are back with us again. Bless you, my dear. Your fever is down today, but you have been really sick with the flu. It's running rampant all through France and England, as if the war wounds weren't enough for us to deal with. They're calling it the Spanish Flu. Not sure why, as it's everywhere in Europe and here in England, too.

"Who are you?"

"My name is Jenny. You and I were going to work on the same ward, but then you took sick as soon as you got here. Not surprising though, 'cos you've been in the field for so long with all those poor blighters in the mud and rain and those fleas and rats ... ooh," she shuddered.

"Can't imagine what it must have been like."

"It was pretty awful."

"Yes, I hear that from the men, too. You were very brave."

"Not really. Just did what we had to do—although it was never enough."

"Well, I heard that when you're stronger, they might send you home, dear. I think you've done more than your share for king and country."

I closed my eyes again. Home! That word sounded wonderful, but what was there for me back home now? I thought about all the years I'd spent with Stephen, growing up together in Victoria, but our real love story only began in wartime, with death all around us. So how could I bear to be in Victoria without him?

The next time Jenny stopped by to check my temperature I tried to sit up. I had begun to feel much stronger.

"Jenny, is this Spanish flu in Canada, too?"

"Yes, I hear it's everywhere around the world. What part of Canada do you come from, Letty?"

"From the west coast—a place called Victoria, in British Columbia."

"Well, I bet you're worried about your family, dear, but there is mail for you, so perhaps it's from your parents—or perhaps a boyfriend?"

"Oh no ... my fiancé was killed in France last year."

"Oh lovey, I'm so sorry—but perhaps there might be a letter from your mum or dad. I'll go and fetch the mail now if you like."

"Yes, please."

I sank back against the pillow, suddenly feeling very weak again. What would the news from home bring? I couldn't bear to hear that anyone was sick—or worse.

And if this beastly flu was in Victoria, maybe I would be needed there now. Nursing others was the only thing I seemed to be good for, and I wanted to do it again.

CHAPTER 11

SARAH (Victoria)

The next months were difficult ones for us all, but we managed somehow to deal with the sadness and grief by being together. Remembering my mother's words, I tried desperately to keep going, for Cal's sake. We talked to him about Stephen a great deal and immortalized him in our memories. He would always be our hero.

In those early days, we had also had a beautiful letter from Letty, who, although devastated by the loss of Stephen, was able to comfort us in our time of sorrow with her words. She vowed she would stay in the field in France or Belgium until this terrible war was over, determined to save as many other young men as she could, for Stephen's sake. We admired her courage and we spent many evenings with Joe and Emily next door, talking about the love our children had had for each other that now would never come to fruition.

Later we heard from Letty again, this time to tell us she was being posted back to England to work in a hospital outside London. We were all relieved and hoped that after that she would return to Victoria.

Sometimes we visited Uncle James and Aunt Eliza's house in James Bay. Their daughter Anna had come over from England at the beginning of the war to stay with them while her husband, Robert, was also serving his country in the navy. Anna and Robert had five children by then, and Anna had matured into a matronly, mature woman, a far cry from her days as a frivolous, flirtatious young girl. The Caldwell homes were always full of boisterous noise, and I noticed that Uncle Edward often escaped the melee to return to his own home or to go over to Providence to spend a quiet evening with my mother.

I prayed that the war would be over long before any of Anna's children were old enough to serve. Meanwhile, their innocent laughter and joy helped us through those dark days. If the war continued much longer, however, I feared that Letty's younger brothers, William and John, might want to volunteer their services. William was already 16, and John would turn 14 at the beginning of 1919. Ernest and I commiserated with their parents over this possibility on a number of occasions. Naturally, they could hardly wait for the safe return of their nursing daughter.

In January of 1918, we were notified by the War Office in London that Stephen had been posthumously awarded the Victoria Cross for his unmitigated bravery in the face of the enemy. His remains would be buried in a cemetery in France and we would be notified of the location. His final act of heroism had helped save the lives of two other young men who were still recovering from their wounds in an English hospital. Stephen had apparently run back into a barrage of shelling to drag them to safety but in the process had lost his own life.

For Ernest and me, this knowledge helped heal our own wounds, and we vowed that after the war was over, we would visit France and the cemetery where he was buried and we would try to find those two men and talk with them, so that we would finally know that Stephen's short life had had a glorious purpose and his sacrifice was worthwhile.

A month later, we received another letter, this time from the Chief of Medical Services at a Canadian field hospital somewhere in France. His name was John McRae. Although dated December of 1917, it did not reach us until early February of 1918.

December 3, 1917
My dear Mr. and Mrs. Hamilton:
The news has only recently reached me here of the death of your son, Stephen. I wish to convey to you my sincere and deepest sympathy.

I knew Steve during the second Battle of Ypres in 1915 and I admired his courage and sensitivity as a wonderful, caring human being. During our short time together, he talked to me of many things—his love for his country, his family and especially for a young lady named Letty. He had a great gift for poetry and the written word and showed me some of his earlier writings. I encouraged him to continue writing, despite all the horrors happening around us, and I could foresee that the world would one day be blessed with a great writer.

But, it was not to be. However, never assume that his life was in vain. I feel I can say this to you with certainty because I know how much he loved and honoured you, his parents.

Soon after my initial meeting with Steve, I was transferred to a field hospital and was moved away from the front. In many ways, I was therefore more fortunate than most, for I was away from the immediate horrors of battle and allowed to care for the wounded from the many skirmishes that followed—the Somme, Vimy Ridge, Arras and Passchendaele.

Last summer I contracted asthma and bronchitis, from which I have never fully recovered—the unpleasant results of that chlorine gas at Ypres! I remember well another dear friend, Alex, who was killed by a shell in May of 1915. Both his death and my meetings with such fine young men as your son Stephen inspired me to write a poem which I am given to understand was published in the British magazine Punch in December of that year.

I would be honoured to enclose a copy of that poem here for you. May it help you both to understand why ordinary men like Stephen go to war—and end up becoming heroes.

In Flanders Fields *
In Flanders fields the poppies blow
Between the crosses, row on row
That mark our place; and in the sky
The larks, still bravely singing, fly
Scarce heard amid the guns below.

We are the Dead. Short days ago
We lived, felt dawn, saw sunset glow,
Loved, and were loved, and now we lie
In Flanders fields.
Take up our quarrel with the foe:
To you from failing hands we throw
The torch; be yours to hold it high.
If ye break faith with us who die
We shall not sleep, though poppies grow
*In Flanders fields. **

May your grief be easier to bear with every day that passes,
Sincerely,
John McCrae.

It was the most beautiful letter of condolence we received, and I vowed to keep it forever. I would save it for Letty to read when she came home and hoped it would bring her the same comfort it had brought to us. We vowed again that one day we would try to find the two young men Stephen had saved from death.

A few weeks later, we were immensely sad to learn that Dr. John McCrae had fallen ill with pneumonia on January 23 and died a few days later at the age of 46, just one short week before his treasured letter had reached us in Victoria.

He was yet another casualty of that beastly war.

CHAPTER 12

The Allied Forces were making great inroads throughout Europe that summer.

Joe and Emily had heard from Letty that she expected to be back in Canada well before Christmas. She had been delayed by a bad case of the influenza when she arrived in England but was now much recovered. We had noticed more and more cases of influenza this year also occurring in Victoria.

The war was now slowly drawing to a close, and much to our delight, Letty came home in August. We were all thrilled to see her, and I begged her for information about everything that she and Stephen had experienced.

I was happy for the Caldwells because they had their daughter home safely, and, talking with Letty and with the support of Ernest and my mother, I managed to finally make my own peace with Stephen's death.

Earlier that year, Ernest had suggested that we should take a trip north to Alaska. The war had affected much of his business affairs in the north, especially since America had joined the war in 1917, and he wanted to settle the affairs of Caldwell, Caldwell & Hamilton. Uncle Edward, now in his eighties, no longer involved himself in the business. The law offices, which had spread and grown through the years, were mainly now run by Ernest, James and Joe Caldwell, but the war had taken its toll on everything in the business world.

We decided we would combine the trip with a visit to Kit Caldwell, who had settled in Alaska since the days of the Klondike Gold Rush. It had been many years since I'd seen Kit, and we were all intrigued to learn that he had finally married and settled down. Even Uncle James and Uncle Edward had not yet met the lady in question, so I readily agreed with Ernest's suggestion. It would be a pleasant diversion from all of our sorrows.

Despite her own advancing years, my mother offered to have Cal stay with her at Providence so Ernest and I could spend a pleasant holiday together, and now that Letty was home, I felt more comfortable about leaving Cal. I was grateful to my mother once again for sensing my need to be with my husband and give him my sole attention.

"We can stay for a month or so, but we will be out of the North before winter and the big freeze sets in, and so will be home well in time for Christmas," said Ernest.

I nodded my agreement. "Yes, a good old-fashioned Christmas will be wonderful, Ernest, with all the Caldwells, McBrides and Hamiltons together at Providence this year. I will suggest it to Mother. It has been far too long, and by then, the war is sure to be over, God willing."

And so on the 17th September, Ernest and I sailed for Skagway in Alaska. Since the United States joined in the Great War in 1917, Skagway had, like many other cities throughout Canada and the States, become a patriotic sea of red, white and blue flags, soldiers in uniform and posters announcing major victories. There were little signs now of the gold rush of the glorious '90s, when Kit Caldwell had first gone there. Most people like Kit, who had made their fortunes in the Klondike, had now invested their money in the towns and cities of Alaska. Kit owned two hotels in Skagway and a great deal of rental real estate besides, plus other property in Dawson City and Juneau. He seemed to have done extremely well for himself.

I recognized his laughing face immediately when he met us at the wharf with enormous bear hugs and then introduced us to his bride, Laura, a bubbly lady of incredible charm. I liked her immediately. Not only was she a beautiful woman, but she possessed a keen sense of humour that matched her husband's. I could see that they were indeed well suited.

"So you finally allowed yourself to get caught, you old reprobate," I said to Kit as I returned his hug with equal enthusiasm. Although he was a few years younger than me, I had always had a soft spot for him. "Laura, how on earth did you manage to tie him down? He's been running from commitment with the ladies for years, and I seem to remember he vowed long ago that he would remain a confirmed bachelor."

"Well," she said, laughing. "I guess I just ran a little faster. And, of course, he just couldn't resist me!"

Kit laughed. "Well, don't you agree she is perfectly irresistible?"

Ernest and I both agreed wholeheartedly as we allowed ourselves and our luggage to be escorted back to Kit and Laura's home on the other side of town.

It was a delightful house, warm, cosy and extremely colourful. Laura obviously loved bright colours around her, because there were splashes of red, orange and green furnishings throughout. "It will help us endure the cold winters," she said laughingly, obviously noticing my initial reaction to all the brilliance. She showed me to the guest room, also decorated in bright greens, while the men went to the den to discuss business.

Once we were alone, she expressed her sympathy about Stephen. "I was so sorry to hear about it, Sarah. It was such a terrible tragedy for you both."

"Yes, it has been hard for us ... but Ernest has been my rock through it all."

She hugged me warmly. There was no pretence about Laura, and it felt as though we had known each other for years. It was almost like finding another friend like Bowery, and before I knew it I found myself opening up to her about losing my beloved father and my best friend all those years ago as well. She in turn confided in me about her life, which had not been an easy one before meeting Kit, whom she obviously adored.

"My childhood was not a happy one," she said. "So Kit and I are determined to make our own family life full of joy. And, the best news of all is that I have just discovered that I am expecting." She beamed. "We must have conceived on our wedding night," she added with a giggle.

"Oh, that's wonderful news! I'm so happy for you."

"Thank you, Sarah. I was reluctant to talk about it to you at first, knowing you have only recently suffered such an awful loss."

"Oh goodness me, no. I would not wish to cast a cloud over your happiness. Having a child, especially your first, is a blessing and a very happy event. Make the most of it."

The one thing I could and would not ever tell her or anyone else about was the circumstances of Stephen's birth. That would remain a secret between my mother and me, a secret we would both take to our graves.

"Tell me about your little son, Cal," Laura then asked.

"Not so little now. He is eight years old and full of mischief. I hope he won't be too much for Mother while we are away, but she has plenty of help at Providence and our nanny has moved in to keep an eye on things, too. Letty is now back in Victoria, as you know, and as a nurse, I'm sure she will keep an eye on everything at Providence. But dear Mama is now in her seventies. She certainly has aged well and still looks like a young woman. She could well be my sister rather than my mother."

"I would love to meet her and see Providence one day," she replied. "The names McBride and Caldwell are well known up here in the North—oh, and Hamilton, of course," she added with a laugh. "But McBride's Transport is something of a legend."

"Yes, my father's early days in British Columbia and up here in Alaska established something of a tradition for travel throughout the west. And I certainly hope you *will* visit us one day and stay with us at

Hamilton House. Once this beastly war is finally over, travelling will be much more fun again."

"And maybe you and Ernest will be blessed with another child, Sarah."

"Goodness me! I'm forty-six, Laura. A little old for childbearing."

"Well, one never knows." She smiled. "This crisp Alaskan air might work wonders for you."

We laughed as we descended the stairs arm in arm to join our husbands. I felt so comfortable with Laura, just as I had with Bowery.

I had once again found a true friend.

* * *

Although we enjoyed the next few weeks, staying with Kit and Laura Caldwell, we were very aware that the North was definitely in decline. The days of the gold rush were long past, and most of the ambitious men who filled the place then had left, taking their dreams of fame and fortune with them. Only the more sensible ones, like Kit Caldwell, had seen other potential in the North and made the most of it.

The majority who lived there now, or who had businesses still operating, did their commerce in Dawson City, Whitehorse or Skagway, but even many of those often headed south for the winter, restricting their commerce to the summer months. Business mainly took place between the break-up of the ice on the Yukon River in May and the beginning of freeze-up in late October.

Ernest and I had planned on leaving Skagway on October 23rd aboard one of the last CP coastal steamers heading south. We tried to persuade the Caldwells to accompany us south for a family visit, but they had already decided they wanted to stay through the winter and await the birth of their first child in the spring before travelling.

Meanwhile, they entertained us royally to a round of sightseeing, visiting, dinners and even balls. For me, it was a most relaxing time, and something I had desperately needed. I missed Cal very much and longed to see him again, but meanwhile Ernest and I grew much closer, so much so that I even began to consider the thought of another child. Forty-six was not too old, surely. I still had my monthly courses, so perhaps it might be possible.

Ernest, of course, was well into his fifties, and we'd had a great deal of trouble conceiving Caleb, but suddenly I felt confident, and when I put the idea to Ernest, much to my surprise, he readily agreed. With an almost impish grin on his dear face, he suggested that we should begin trying that very night. And so we did.

The next morning, as I sat at the dressing-table mirror brushing my hair, I felt warm and at peace with myself. Ernest stood behind me and then bent to kiss my bare shoulders.

"I love you, Sarah," he said. "I cannot begin to tell you just how much."

"I think, my love, you showed me quite adequately last night."

"Oh dear, do you think we made too much noise? Maybe our hosts will suspect something was going on." He laughed.

"Only that we are very much in love and not too old to show it."

Later, on my own, I talked to Bowery, as I was apt to do sometimes. I still felt her presence around me and felt sure she could hear me. *Bowery*, I said. *I think I have finally found my one true passion in life. And isn't it ridiculous? It was here, right in front of my eyes all the time ...*

Wherever she was now, I knew Bowery would understand.

* * *

Three days before our departure, we were all invited to an end-of-the-season ball in Juneau, the capital city of Alaska since 1906, when the government had been transferred from Sitka. Kit explained a little of Juneau's history as we journeyed there in his motor car on the day before the ball.

"This whole area was originally the fishing grounds for the Tlingit indigenous people," he said, "but in the late 1800s it created a great deal of attention when a Tlingit named Kowee found gold ore samples in response to a reward offered by George Pilz, an engineer in Sitka. Realizing the potential for a gold strike, in August of 1880, Pilz himself grubstaked two prospectors, Richard Harris and Joseph Juneau, in order to find more gold. And more gold they did indeed find in Gold Creek, but unfortunately they didn't follow the gold to its source. Kowee kept insisting there must be more, so finally Pilz dispatched the two prospectors back to the area. Once they had climbed Snow Slide Gulch at the head of Gold Creek, they found themselves looking down on the mother lode itself, at Quartz Gulch and Silver Bow Basin. On October 18th, they staked out a 160-acre town site on the beach and a month later joined boatloads of other prospectors all travelling to the new strike on the Gastineau Channel. Before long, a stampede had begun. That discovery, in fact, was actually the first to result in the founding of an Alaskan town, and Juneau quickly grew from there. The rest is history."

"My goodness, Kit, you are so knowledgeable about the history of Alaska," I said with a smile.

"Well, it has become my home now, and I love it."

"I can see that. You even talk with a twang like the Americans!"

Kit laughed out loud. "Oh, heaven forbid! I can just hear your dear mother's voice now telling you and the twins, and all of us Caldwells, that we should always keep our British accents. 'Don't ever develop that awful twang the Americans use,' she would say. Remember?"

Ernest and I laughed. "Oh yes, indeed. And she tells Cal that all the time. She still speaks with her perfect upper-class English accent, which she cultivated as a child I think, even though she didn't grow up in a wealthy, elite family."

The ball was being held at the most prestigious Golden Lights Hotel, and anyone who was anyone attended that night. It was to be a final farewell to the North for many politicians and businessmen before heading south for the winter.

It was also the first formal event Ernest and I had attended in a long while. The gloom of the war years, followed by Stephen's death, had left us both unwilling to indulge in any such frivolities, but that night, with news that the war was almost over, everyone seemed to be in a carefree mood.

CHAPTER 13

The orchestra was playing a Strauss waltz, one that Mother often played on the piano. I looked across the room at some people who had just arrived, and suddenly I saw him. The years fell away, and once again I was young, remembering how fiercely attracted I had once been to him in a single moment in time.

We were both older now—he in his mid-fifties, with grey streaks wandering through his black hair. But for a brief second he still made my heart beat a little faster. And he looked so much like Papa it was almost frightening. I felt sure that anyone who had known my father would realize that he was his son.

"Goodness," I heard Kit saying to my left. "Look, Sarah, isn't that that fellow Etienne Dupont who came to Victoria once, looking for funds for an expedition to the Hudson's Bay? I remember hearing through the years that he had done very well and made pots of money. I heard he lives somewhere in Ontario but visits Alaska on occasion. Let's go over and make ourselves known."

I hesitated. "I think not, Kit. After all, it was a long time ago. I'd rather dance with my husband."

"Oops, I just remembered, Ernest. I think Dupont was rather sweet on you, Sarah. Sorry, I'd forgotten."

"Oh, don't be ridiculous, Kit. He was nothing of the sort. Come on, Ernest, please dance with me."

And with that, he swung me around the floor in a waltz. But I knew that Etienne had seen me. He was watching us both intensely, hardly aware of the lady on his own arm. When the music finally stopped and I caught my breath again, I saw that he and his partner were heading toward us.

"Mademoiselle McBride," he said, bowing formally. "How nice to see you again."

"Mr. Dupont, isn't it?" I replied, slightly flustered. "Yes ... very nice, but I am now Mrs. Hamilton and this is my husband, Ernest. Oh, and you remember Kit Caldwell, no doubt. And this is his wife, Laura."

Etienne bowed to everyone and then introduced the lady on his arm. "This is my wife, Julia."

She smiled a smile that was rather insipid, I thought—or was I just being particularly catty? Etienne could have done a whole lot better.

"May I borrow your wife, Mr. Hamilton, for the next dance?" Etienne suddenly asked.

Ernest seemed unaware of any undertones and readily agreed. "Only if you allow me the pleasure of dancing with your wife, Mr. Dupont," he replied.

"Of course."

And so, after an interval of almost twenty years, I was once more in his arms, and we were gazing into each other's eyes. But I knew there was nothing there any more, other perhaps than a natural affection, given the nature of our true relationship. But there was no blinding attraction. No uncontrollable passion. Nothing. And for that I was grateful. I knew in that moment that I was over him, and that I truly did love Ernest.

"Sarah, I ... I am so glad to see you again and to know you are ... happy?" He made the statement sound like a question.

"Yes, Etienne, I am very happy."

"I trust that means that you forgave me all those years ago."

"Forgave you? For what?"

"For leaving as I did."

And then, of course, I realized he still believed that I thought he had merely deserted me.

"Etienne, I do know the truth," I whispered. "I knew it almost from the start."

He stared at me in amazement. "Oh my God. I prayed you would never find out. I would rather have had you believe I was just a rotten cad. But how? How did you find out?"

"I overheard a conversation between my mother and Uncle Edward. You know me, I always was inquisitive. I loved to listen in to other people's conversations. Look where it got me."

"Ah Sarah, I'm so terribly sorry."

"Me too," I gulped. "But ... there you are. Nobody's fault. Life goes on. And what about you? Are you happy, Etienne?"

He sighed. "It took me a long time, Sarah. I thought I might become a priest in the beginning."

I threw my head back and laughed. "Oh Etienne, a priest? You? No, never!"

"Well, as you can see, I didn't follow that ridiculous idea. Instead I indulged myself with a great many women, but no one filled the empty space. No one."

"What about Julia?" I nodded toward his wife who, although dancing with Ernest, was studying us both closely.

"Julia? We married about six years ago. I met her in New York. Her family owns one of the largest fur houses there. Our marriage was also a good business union, and we're reasonably happy together. Our lifestyles are compatible."

"Oh, Etienne, that sounds so cold."

"Not really! We have a good life, and now I am content knowing that you are happily married. Do you have any children?"

This was the moment I had dreaded. I would never tell him that our union had produced Stephen. Never. Stephen was dead now, so it hardly mattered.

"Yes, Etienne," I replied. "Ernest and I were blessed with two sons, but we lost one in the Great War." I continued talking quickly before he had a chance to reply or ask any questions. "Our little boy, Cal, is now eight years old and is being taken care of by my mother while we're away. We leave for Victoria on the 23rd and are very anxious to see him again."

"I'm sure ... and your ... father? I heard that he died a few years ago. I'm so sorry."

"Yes, Etienne ... he died in 1898. He had suffered with stomach cancer and was in great pain. It was a happy release, in the end." I paused, remembering that unhappy time once again, before adding with finality, "*Our* father died in 1898."

Finally, the words had been spoken. The music drifted to a close, and he escorted me back to Ernest. "It was a pleasure to meet you, Mr. Hamilton," he said. "Forgive me for monopolizing your wife, but we had some catching up to do. I wish you both a pleasant and safe journey back to Victoria."

We said our goodbyes and he and Julia crossed the room to rejoin their own party. Ernest waltzed me away again as the music began once more.

"That was him, wasn't it Sarah?" he asked, after a moment of silence.

"Him? Who?"

"The man you fell in love with before me. Stephen's biological father?"

"Oh Ernest, please. It was so long ago. I am over that now. You know that."

"Yes, my dearest wife, I do know that. I know beyond a shadow of a doubt that you truly love me now, but it has taken you a long, long time to reach this point. I think I am right about that, aren't I?"

"Yes, my love, you are. Thank you, Ernest.

"For what, dearest?"

"For being you and for understanding, and for all the wonderful things you have brought to my life. For everything. What did I ever do to deserve you?"

"Just pure McBride luck, I guess," he said with a grin, as we continued waltzing in each other's arms.

That night, back at the hotel, I wrote a long letter to my mother, telling her of our wonderful holiday and that we would be sailing home on the 23rd. Ernest had already notified the McBride's shipping office in Victoria, so Bertie would already know of our arrival date. But for some reason, I needed my mother to know how happy I was.

I was suddenly so content with my life, more so than I had ever been in the past. Everything had come full circle. All my past misdemeanours were cleared up and accounted for, so I told her about my meeting with Etienne. And I told her of my true feelings for Ernest. I wanted her to share my happiness, but, most of all, I wanted her to know how very much I loved her.

I now understood so many things about my life. It was as though I had been granted some divine understanding of all life's mysteries. Even Stephen's death seemed preordained, and I was finally at peace with my past. I hoped that letter to my mother would fully convey all those feelings.

The next morning, we returned to Skagway with Kit and Laura, and on the 23rd October we bade them a sad farewell at the wharf before boarding the CP Coastal Steamer the *Princess Sophia.*

It was beginning to snow lightly as we cleared the dock around noon and set sail on the last run of the season, south on a journey to Vancouver, Victoria and Seattle. Ernest and I were two of the 343 people aboard, all escaping the North for a warmer climate.

I couldn't wait to get home and see Cal again.

CHAPTER 14

LETTY

Soon after Sarah and Ernest left for the North, I asked if I might move into Providence because I wanted to help Granny Mac with Cal.

I thought he might be too much for her, even though his nanny was there with him and Granny Mac also had her dear companion Dulcie to help. But Dulcie was about Granny Mac's age and hadn't been herself since her husband, Skip, had passed away the year before. So I reasoned that I would be needed, and, truth be told, I just wanted to be near little Cal. He was such a dear and I enjoyed his company. He became like the son I had never had, and in many ways he reminded me of Stephen.

I also continued to work shifts at the hospital, because the Spanish flu was becoming rampant in Victoria by then. Everywhere I went, people were wearing masks, and I feared that, even though I was very careful, I might spread the virus to everyone at Providence. I thought that maybe I should move back home, but then, a few days later, Granny Mac developed a bad cough and I decided to stop working at the hospital and just take care of her, in case she developed this beastly flu.

I insisted she stay in complete isolation in her room and have all her meals brought to her. I was the only one allowed to be near her. Because of her age, I feared this particular virus might do irreparable damage to her health.

"Oh, you fuss far too much, Letty," she croaked between coughing bouts. "I assure you I am not going to let the flu kill me. If I can survive scrubbing floors until my hands were red, being beaten nearly to death, being violated, travelling for three months on a voyage to hell, having two miscarriages and losing my beloved little son, my husband and my grandson, I can assure you that the flu won't kill me now."

I stared at her in amazement. *What did she just say?* I knew nothing about her past and how she originally came to Victoria from England. All I knew was that she was a governess and had become governess to my grandfather but—scrubbing floors, being beaten and being *raped?* Did she really just tell me that? Maybe I had misheard.

"Granny Mac, whatever do you mean?"

"Oh, forget all that. I just meant that a silly flu bug won't destroy me now—that's all."

I was sure she was regretting having said all that and wanted to change the subject quickly, so I replied, "Of course not, dear, but we have to take these precautions and be safe."

"But I want to see Cal, so you'll have to move my bed nearer the window so I can watch him while he's playing in the garden."

I agreed to do this to ensure she would stay in bed, so with some difficulty I pushed her bed across the floor to the window.

"Why do you wear that silly mask, Letty?" she said. "I want to see your pretty face."

"I have to wear it, Granny Mac. It's mandatory, and that is why I'm keeping others away from you while you are contagious."

She tutted impatiently.

"Ah ... there he is. My little grandson."

We both watched Cal as he kicked a ball around on the grass. Granny Mac tapped on the window until he looked up and waved.

"Hello, Granny Mac," he shouted. "Are you feeling better yet?"

I opened the window just a crack and called back to him. "Your Granny is making good progress, Cal. She wanted to watch you play, so I moved her bed to the window."

He beamed from ear to ear. "Yippee, that's super duper! Watch how high I can kick the ball, Gran."

"What a dear boy he is, Letty, but I do wish he would try to speak the King's English. He's picking up all those terrible American slang expressions. We'll have to put a stop to that."

I smiled as I closed the window. She was definitely feeling better.

* * *

True to form, Granny Mac fully recovered within a week and joined us again for meals.

"I told you, Letty. It would take more than the Spanish flu to finish me off," she said.

"Well, we're all very pleased to see you are so much better now, dear."

Uncle Bertie and Uncle Teddy agreed with me, and I was glad that they had avoided the flu. It seemed it was affecting younger people more than the elderly,

"I'm sure you're needed back at the hospital now, Letty," Granny Mac said. "I think you'd better return to work, but I do appreciate all that you did for me—and for helping with Cal. And you can move back home and take care of your parents, in case they develop the flu."

I agreed with her. It was the sensible thing to do, but I hated the thought of moving away from Providence. There were way too many memories of Stephen at my parents' house, as my childhood with Stephen had been spent at our two houses, side by side. And I hated the way my mother and father watched me all the time, as though expecting me to collapse in a heap of grief at any moment.

Nonetheless, I knew it was time I moved on with my life, and I knew I could always visit Cal at any time. As it happened, I would be very glad I had returned to my parents' house, because a few days later, a visitor arrived at Hamilton House next door.

A visitor who would change my life.

CHAPTER 15

I was working in the garden, clipping off the last of the dead roses. I loved our garden next door to Hamilton House, because it reminded me of Stephen and how we had played there so very long ago. Something made me look up, and through the hedge I saw a motor car pull up in the driveway next door.

A man in uniform got out of the car and stood for a moment, talking to the driver. He seemed to be finding his balance and, as he walked slowly toward the front door, I realized why. The driver had handed him crutches. His right leg was missing.

For one ludicrous moment I thought it was Stephen—but I knew that was impossible. Stephen had died two years ago. But this man looked somewhat like him and wore a similar uniform. Once he removed his hat, I could see he also had dark, wavy hair like Stephen's. He was about to ring the doorbell, and I couldn't resist calling out.

"Hello there," I said. "I'm afraid the Hamiltons are away right now. Can I help you?"

"Oh dear, I should have telephoned before calling," he said as he turned and slowly hobbled toward me. "My name is Austin Harris ..."

Suddenly I felt faint. I began to sway. I knew that name, because I'd heard it before.

"Are you all right, miss?"

"Yes, yes, of course. It's just that ..."

"Oh my God. Are you Letty Caldwell?"

I nodded.

"I'm so sorry. My arrival here must have been a shock for you. But I wanted to meet Stephen's parents—and you—to let you know that I was the one whose life Stephen saved at Courcelette. He is the reason I am here today."

I could barely speak, but I managed to mumble a few words. "Yes, they told us the names of the men he ..."

"Miss Caldwell, he was very brave. He was so ill and almost dying, but he ran out and dragged me and another chap back behind the lines. Then he collapsed, and ..."

"Died?"

He nodded.

"What happened to the other chap?"

"Well, apparently we were both taken to a nearby hospital and then sent back to England. I had to have my right leg amputated, and Charlie was blinded by the shell explosion and lost an arm. Stephen was the leader of our unit. He was always talking about you, Miss Caldwell. He loved you very much."

"Thank you for coming, Mr. Harris. The Hamiltons will be so sorry to have missed you, but they will be home next week from Alaska. Are you in town for long?"

"Yes, I've been shipped here to the rehabilitation hospital at Craigdarroch Castle, where I'm now staying. I'm doing physiotherapy there now, and they are going to try and fit one of those artificial legs onto my stump. But I wanted to meet you and Stephen's parents, to tell you how brave your fiancé was. He saved my life that day, and I am eternally grateful. Charlie is, too, but he's now back in Toronto with his family. He never recovered his sight."

"Oh, I'm so sorry. Where are you from, Mr. Harris?"

"My family is in Calgary."

"Do you have a wife there?"

"Oh no, just my parents and a sister back there." He paused. "Steve was such a great chap. We had long talks in which he told me about you. I know you are a nurse. He said you planned to marry ..."

"He was a kind man." My voice broke. I realized that Austin Harris would probably leave soon, and for some reason I wanted him to stay, and to talk to him some more.

"Mr. Harris, would you like to come inside to meet my mother? My father is at work but should be home soon. I am sure we can rustle up some tea for you, and I know they would love to meet you, too."

He smiled, a smile that comforted me. "I would love that, Miss Caldwell."

"Please call me Letty."

"Only if you'll call me Austin."

I returned his smile. "Of course. Come this way, Austin."

He asked his driver to wait and followed me inside. My mother was delighted to meet Austin, and we sat in the living room drinking tea and reminiscing about Stephen. When my father arrived, he insisted that Austin stay for dinner, so I offered to tell his driver to leave and return at nine o'clock.

It was so comforting to talk to someone who had been with Stephen at the end. It didn't make the pain go away, but it certainly eased it.

* * *

Before he left, I told Austin I would visit him at the hospital the next day, and he seemed pleased.

"There's some pretty awful sights there, Letty, but I suppose you're used to that, being a nurse."

I nodded. "Yes I am. I am still nursing here, at the Jubilee. But I will enjoy seeing you make progress with your physiotherapy—and maybe I can help. I can volunteer there, too, as I'm sure they need volunteers."

My mother looked at me strangely. I couldn't decide if she was pleased or puzzled by my announcement.

Over the next couple of days, I visited Austin at the rehabilitation hospital a number of times and saw the excellent work they were doing there. By volunteering in rehab as well as doing my shifts at the Jubilee, I was very tired at the end of each day, but at least I had more opportunities to sit with Austin and chat.

Slowly he began to make me laugh again, and I couldn't wait for the Hamiltons to get home and meet him in two days. It would comfort them so much. In many ways, he reminded me of Stephen, and I think they would see that, too.

One afternoon we sat on the lawn outside the hospital, looking up toward the castle. The castle and surrounding grounds had been converted into a makeshift hospital, and the view all around was spectacular.

"Had you been inside the castle in its heyday, Letty?" he asked suddenly.

"Oh yes—a few times, when I was small and the Dunsmuir family owned it. I don't really remember it much, but I think Stephen's mother was a bridesmaid to one of their daughters—or maybe it was the other way around. I can't really recall what I was told. It was so long ago."

"How very grand. Your family must be very important in Victoria, to have socialized with people who own a castle."

I laughed. "Oh goodness, no, Austin. The Caldwells and the McBrides were important at one time, but things have changed so much since the turn of the century and then since the war. We would now be termed as 'old money,' I suppose—even the Dunsmuirs."

"Well I'm still very impressed, and once I've got used to my artificial leg and climbing steps again, I'd like to go inside the castle when it's no longer a hospital."

"I'd love to take you," I replied. Then I blushed, thinking I may have assumed too much.

"I hope so," he said. And then added, "And I'd love to take you back to Calgary to visit my family, Letty."

"And you must come and see Providence. That's where Stephen's grandmother lives. She would definitely want to meet you, Austin."

We gazed at each other for a moment and then quickly looked away, as though we both wondered what exactly we had just said.

In any event, I didn't think about it anymore, because two days later, on the morning of October 26, all hell broke loose at Providence and I completely forgot about Austin and the friendship we had begun to form out of so much heartache and tragedy.

My only thought was for Granny Mac and little Cal.

CHAPTER 16

JANE

"Granny Mac. Look! Look! Way up there. See the eagle. It's circling round and round."

"I see it, Cal. It's beautiful."

"I shall fly like that one day, Granny Mac. I shall be right up there with the eagles, just you wait and see."

I laughed at his youthful enthusiasm as he ran across the lawn at Providence looking skyward on that October day. He was so innocent and sublimely happy, but he was obsessed with those wretched flying machines and most of the time talked of nothing else.

The afternoon held a nip in the air, a portent of winter ahead. Sarah and Ernest would be home soon, and Cal would be so happy to see them, but, oh how I had enjoyed his company during the weeks they had been gone. He was such a bright little boy, so full of life and energy. He made me feel young again, and I know that both Bertie and Teddy enjoyed having him around.

If only he wouldn't keep talking about flying. It seemed such a dangerous activity to me, and I could not imagine why anyone would want to fly up in the sky in those terrible machines, taking their very lives in their hands. However, I hated to discourage him.

"I'm sure you will fly one day, dear," I replied, thinking inwardly that we would all face that problem if and when it ever happened. My attention, however, was suddenly diverted by the arrival of Bertie driving up to the house at rather a reckless speed and pulling to an abrupt halt by the front door. It reminded me again that Bertie was really the only one who encouraged Cal's obsession with the air. He also believed that flying might one day be a regular alternative means of transportation and something McBride's should look into!

"Ooh, it's Uncle Bertie, goodie, goodie," said Cal, having also spotted his uncle. "I want to show him the model airplane I made."

It was unusual for Bertie to come home at this time of day. He rarely broke away from his office routine, so I was surprised to see him. I was even more surprised when he began to run toward me across the lawn with an anxious expression on his face.

"Bertie, hello dear. What is it? You look concerned."

"Mother, I have news ... oh, Cal, hello."

"Uncle Bertie, you're home early. That's good, 'cos I have something to show you. It's up in my room and it's just wonderful."

"Well, maybe you should run up there right now and get it, Cal. I want to talk with your grandmother for a moment, anyway."

"All right," he said happily, unaware of his uncle's somewhat grim expression. "Wait right here and I'll bring it down."

Once he was out of earshot, Bertie took my arm. "Mother, I have had some disturbing news about the *Princess Sophia*. It left Skagway at noon yesterday and sailed headlong into a storm. The news is coming through slowly and is still very sketchy but ..."

"But what, Bertie? What has happened? Please God, tell me it isn't bad news."

"I don't know for sure, Mother. I'm in constant touch with Captain Troup at the CP office here in Victoria, and his counterparts in Skagway and Juneau, but it doesn't sound good. I'm going right back there now, but I wanted to be sure that Teddy was home here with you and Cal when we get more definite news."

"Teddy? No, dear, he's out on a call. Mrs. Harrison's baby is due any time and he went over there ... but why? Tell me exactly what you have heard."

"The ship ran aground in the Lynn Canal in a blinding snowstorm. They believe it struck Vanderbilt Reef in the middle of the night and is still lodged there."

"Oh dear God, no, Bertie. No."

"There is no word of injuries among passengers or crew, Mother, and apparently there are many rescue vessels in the area already, so let's not assume the worst. Here is a copy of the message, which arrived a short while ago at the CP office."

He handed me the paper which simply read: *Princess Sophia ran aground on Vanderbilt Reef. Ship not taking any water. Unable to back off at high water. Fresh northerly wind. Ship pounding. Assistance on way from Juneau.*

"Oh, my poor Sarah, and Ernest. How frightened they must be."

"They will be rescued, I'm sure, Mother. Just hold on." He squeezed my hand, but I knew he also was very worried. Cal was now running toward us, clasping his precious model in his hand. "No word to the boy yet, Mother. Not until we know they are safe."

"No, of course not ... of course not."

"Well, what have you there, young man?" said Bertie.

"It's my latest model, Uncle Bertie. I copied it from a picture in my air machines book. It's a Curtiss flyer. What do you think?"

"I think it is very fine, Cal, and I will examine it more closely later, but right now I have to hurry back to the office on important business. I want you to stay here with your grandmother until I get home again, and then we'll take a closer look together."

Then, turning to me, he added, "Mother, I will telephone you with the latest news, and when Teddy gets back, tell him to stay home if possible until there is word."

"Yes, dear," I said, wondering how I would get through the coming hours, trying to stay positive and pretending nothing was amiss in front of Cal.

Bertie hurried off, and Cal and I went back inside, where I asked Mrs. Stapleton to prepare some tea. I didn't feel like eating or drinking, but I knew I must do something to keep my mind off the events that might be taking place on the *Princess Sophia*.

When Teddy arrived home an hour later, it was apparent that he had already heard the news. While Cal was occupied at play, he whispered his concerns to me. "Mother, we must not think the worst. Bertie managed to contact me at the Harrisons, and he said the news is still the same. Rescue boats are plying their way through the area, and they expect that all passengers will be transferred into the lifeboats soon."

"But the storm, Teddy? It's a really bad one, isn't it?"

"Yes, but Bertie says that the captain, Captain Locke, is apparently a fine fellow and knows what he's doing. He has instructed all the rescue boats to stand by and await the next tide, when he hopes to release all the passengers. Mother, all is not lost."

"I know, Teddy. Sarah will be home again safely, I'm sure."

Although McBride's Transportation had extricated itself from most of its shipping interests following Gideon's death and the Canadian Pacific monopoly on the west coast, Bertie was still kept apprised of all seafaring activity in the area and had a number of contacts. I knew he would be able to easily keep up on events as things unfolded.

Teddy then went over to Cal to keep him distracted, and I continued to stare at the telephone, willing it to ring with good news from Bertie. I knew that by now the *Princess Sophia* had been grounded for many hours, and darkness would soon be falling again. That biting north wind and blinding snow would be unbearable.

The telephone finally rang, its loud trill startling me and interrupting my thoughts.   "Bertie?" I snapped into the mouthpiece.

"Yes, Mother. I've just got the latest. Captain Locke has told all the rescue fleet to head for shelter tonight, and they will attempt a rescue again at first light. It is best that way, and they will stand a better chance, once the storm lessens."

"Oh Bertie, are there signs of it abating? What are we to do?"

"Try to get some rest now, Mother. Put Cal to bed, and we will all pray. I'm staying here at the CP office all night."

"All right, dear. Call us ... the minute you hear anything."

And then the long vigil began.

CHAPTER 17

Bertie phoned us at dawn with news that the CP manager Troup had received a wire from the *Princess Sophia* to send all possible salvage gear to the area. Lifeboats were at the ready and, although the seas were still heavy, he believed that rescue would soon be negotiated.

Teddy and I prayed those words were true as we ate a scant breakfast. Cal was still sleeping, and I did not intend to wake him.

"Mother, I think I should give you a mild sedative," said Teddy. "The strain is becoming too much for you."

"I will not take anything until I know they are safe, so stop behaving like a doctor and just behave like my son instead."

But as the day progressed, the news grew worse. Word came through from other ships in the area that the storm had rebuilt and had now reached gale force again. Many of the smaller vessels had taken shelter along the coast, unable to reach the *Princess Sophia*. The Lynn Canal had become a nightmare.

The next news received in Victoria at the CP office announced that the *Princess Sophia* was floundering on the reef. There was little hope of saving her or her passengers in the chaos that followed.

I don't know at what point that day I finally realized my daughter and son-in-law might be dead. I just know that it was early on the morning of October 26th that we were told a lull in the storm had enabled other ships to reach the area and approach the infamous Vanderbilt Reef. By then, all that remained of the *Princess Sophia* was about twenty feet of mast showing above sea level.

When an exhausted Bertie arrived home to tell me the news, I think I screamed. *It could not be true! Not Sarah! Not Ernest!* How could I bear this latest horror, and how could I possibly tell their small son that, in one horrific moment in time, he had lost both his parents? Wasn't it only two years ago that he had also lost his beloved older brother?

God, why have you forsaken us? Are the McBrides truly forever doomed? Are we destined never to be happy for long?

During the hours that followed, I think Edward, James, Eliza, Joe, Emily and Letty all arrived at Providence. I just know that the house suddenly seemed full of Caldwells. I don't really know who they all were. But they were all whispering. Why were they whispering? And Dulcie and Mrs. Stapleton were fussing around us all with tea and sandwiches, while trying to hold back their own tears.

Joe, Emily and Letty finally offered to take Cal home with them for the night while we discussed how best he should be told. Bertie and Teddy said they would speak with him the next day. I knew I simply could not bear to break that little boy's heart once again.

Finally, I allowed Teddy to give me a sedative because I wanted to sink into oblivion. I thought that maybe the nightmare would be gone when I awoke.

* * *

The house was quiet now. Would there ever be noise and laughter again?

I opened my eyes, and it was morning. A tap came at the door and it opened slowly. Dulcie stood there, holding a breakfast tray.

"Mr. Bertie asked me to bring this in to you, Miss Jane. You must eat something. Both he and Mr. Teddy want to talk to you. They said, once you're awake."

"As you can see, Dulcie, I'm awake. Has everyone else left?"

"Mr. Edward Caldwell is downstairs still, in the library. He stayed here the night. And I think Mr. and Mrs. Joe Caldwell returned a while ago, with Miss Letty and young Mr. Cal."

"Good. Dulcie, I can't eat. Just help me dress and I'll come downstairs."

"But, Miss Jane ..."

"I'll eat something later, to appease you all. Why do these awful things keep happening to us, Dulcie? I have lost so many loved ones, and you have lost your dear Skiff. It doesn't make any sense."

"But we always got through it together," she replied. "Death never makes sense when it happens to the young, but grief is the price we pay for love, I suppose."

"You are so very wise," I replied as I got out of bed and she fussed around me while I washed and dressed, complaining all the time that my body needed sustenance. I knew she was right, because I could not remember when last I had eaten and I admit I felt very weak. But I was worried about Cal and I needed to talk to the twins. And, most of all, I needed to speak with Edward. He was always so strong and supportive at these times, just like my Gideon had been. *Oh Gideon, how I need you now*, I whispered.

As I entered the library where they were all gathered, Bertie took both my hands and pulled me to him in a hug.

"Mother," he simply said.

Then Teddy kissed my cheek and Edward put his arms around me and we swayed together, like two floundering old souls.

"Is Cal in his room?

They nodded. "We have told him," said Teddy. "He's with Uncle James and Aunt Eliza, but he asked for you, Mother."

"I'll go to him at once—"

"Just wait a moment, Mother," said Teddy. "We had to break it gently ..."

"Well, of course. Did you imagine I would be harsh with him?"

"Of course not, Mother, but to begin with, we have just said the ship had run aground and that they were trying to rescue all the passengers."

"Which was true."

"And ... we sort of ..."

"You mean he hasn't been told the latest news—that all hope is lost and the *Princess Sophia* has sunk."

Bertie shrugged. "The rescue ships have returned to the area and are now retrieving bodies. They will be taken to Juneau or Skagway, where the *Princess Alice* is awaiting them for transportation south and for identification. But there could still be survivors, mother. Miracles do happen."

"Miracles! Oh Bertie, I prayed there would be a miracle, but please be honest with me. We cannot hold out false hope for that little boy, can we?"

"No."

"Then I will tell Cal the whole truth. Sooner or later, he has to know. There is no point in delaying. I am the one who must do it. Last night I had ... I had to do my own grieving. I could not have told him then."

"We'll come with you, Mother."

Letty spoke up, too. "I'll come too, Granny Mac. I'm used to telling people bad news."

"Yes, Letty. You may come up with me, and you, too, Edward, but no one else ... I must see my grandson now."

So Edward, Letty and I slowly ascended the stairs to Cal's room. It seemed to me then that we were like old soldiers who had weathered many a storm, but this perhaps would prove to be the worst.

CHAPTER 18

Cal's eyes opened wide in horror. "But Granny, how can a big ship like that sink?"

"The storm was very strong, Cal."

"Where did all the people go? To the bottom of the ocean?"

Edward held my hand tightly. "No, Cal," I replied. "The rescue boats would have picked them up."

"So Mumsy and Pops might be saved and will come home again?"

I shook my head sadly. "The word this morning is that no one survived, dear."

"*Survived*? You mean they are all *dead*! Mumsy and Pops and everyone are all dead?"

I nodded. The lump in my throat made it impossible to speak, so Letty took over for me. "You must be brave now, Caleb. It is terrible news to have to hear, but—yes—it looks like no one survived, I'm afraid." I was near to tears.

But that sweet little boy simply rushed into my arms and said, "Oh Granny, I'm so sorry for you."

I looked at Edward. How could Caleb still manage to comfort me when he had just lost both his parents in one terrible moment of horror?

"And I for you, Cal."

"We must be brave and strong for one another, Granny Mac. I know how sad you must be."

I nodded again. He then hugged Letty.

"Cal, you are such a brave young man," said Edward, taking the boy in his arms. "We will all be strong for one another."

Ever curious, Cal then asked, "Will their bodies come home? And will we have to bury them up at St. Luke's and have a ceremony, like we had for Steve? They never sent his body home, did they? They just said he was in Flanders Field."

I was astounded that he remembered and understood so much. He was only eight years old. "They are retrieving people from the waters, dear. When they bring them south, Uncle Bertie says we will have to identify them, and then we can place them at rest at St. Luke's, and you can visit your Mumsy and Pops up there."

"But they will be dead, Granny, right? Their souls will be in heaven, won't they?"

"Yes, my love, their souls will be in heaven."

That night, Cal had a violent nightmare, and he rushed screaming into my room. "They're drowning, Granny! They're drowning! Help them, please. The water is so cold."

It was only the first of many such nightmares in the weeks that followed, but during the daytime hours he remained the stoic, brave, little eight-year-old boy that he always was.

He was a boy that had been thrust into such unbearable sorrow and loss, and my heart broke for him.

* * *

On November 8, three days before Armistice was declared, the *Princess Alice* began her slow and painful journey south, carrying a cargo of 159 caskets. She was dubbed the Ship of Sorrows. Her first stop was Vancouver on November 11, and then she travelled to Victoria before finally heading for Seattle.

As she entered Victoria Harbour, her flag flew at half-mast, and we were informed that she would dispose of twenty-five caskets covered in black crepe at the Victoria Canadian Pacific warehouse for identification. These were the passengers it was assumed were from Victoria, but no one knew for sure. If we were not able to identify Sarah or Ernest among those twenty-five, Bertie had arranged for us to travel to Vancouver to see if any bodies there remained unidentified. If not, we would travel to Seattle. If we still had not found our loved ones, we would have to admit they might be among those who were still being washed up on the beaches of the west coast.

The gruesome task for our family began at eight o'clock in the morning of November 13. The *Princess Alice* had slipped into harbour late on the afternoon of the 12th, unnoticed by the jubilant crowds still celebrating the end of the Great War. They had gathered in Beacon Hill Park or lined Government Street on Armistice Day and were still revelling in their newfound freedom. The war was finally over, and the celebrations would continue for days.

Newspaper headlines two weeks earlier had told the tragic story of the *Princess Sophia,* with headlines announcing *Passengers Still on Board,* then *Wind in Lynn Canal Prevents Transfer from the Princess Sophia,* and finally *All is Lost. Princess Sophia gone.* But in essence the news of the greatest loss of life in a marine disaster on the northwest coast had been overshadowed by the celebrations marking the end of the Great War.

After four years of unmitigated sorrow and loss of life in Europe, people were now clamouring for happy news. They did not want to wallow in more misery, and I could hardly blame them. Only those of us directly involved in the tragedy were a part of the unfolding horror in that cold Canadian Pacific warehouse on that wretched morning in November.

As we entered the building, I was flanked by my sons, who kept insisting that I should not be subjected to this task. "Teddy and I could do it quite easily, Mother. You should have stayed at home."

"Bertie," I replied, "I have to find her, don't you understand? I have to know for sure."

They both nodded sombrely as we joined the procession passing before the open caskets. The bodies looked unreal. Some embalming had obviously been performed in Juneau or Skagway, so most of the results of their sea horror had been obliterated. Now there were just blank, white faces, eyes closed, and a faint smell of oil everywhere. The boilers on the *Princess Sophia* had exploded at the end, we were told, so oil had seeped into the turbulent waters and covered the bodies. I fervently hoped that both Sarah and Ernest had died instantly. I could not bear the thought of them being burned in the ship's fire, or gasping for breath as they drowned, or being frozen by the icy waters or ...

One face after another. To me, they all looked the same. Unreal. These were not people—they were just alabaster models. Would I recognize my beautiful daughter?

"Oh Bertie, Teddy," I whispered. "This is too awful."

"Come Mother, come and sit down. Teddy and I will finish."

"*No!* Not yet."

And then I saw her. She did look different from the rest, but in what way I could not say. She was still my daughter, but her face was lifeless. No expression—all the buoyancy and joy had gone. Was she at peace, I wondered.

I did not want to see her this way. No, I wanted to remember her instead as a little barefooted girl, jumping from a canoe with sand all over her; or a young schoolgirl dressed in her prim and proper uniform, or a beautiful young woman curtsying to the Queen, and then, most of all, I wanted to remember her as she was on her wedding day, descending the stairs at Providence, so exquisitely beautiful, an Ice Maiden.

I also remembered her despair when Etienne had left her, and then the horror of knowing about their true relationship when she overheard my discussion with Edward.

And I could still recall the expression on her face as she held Stephen for the first time after he was born. I revelled in the memory of that maternal glow on her lovely face.

Isn't he beautiful, mother? Isn't he the most beautiful baby you've ever seen?

I remembered her grief at Gideon's funeral, when she sobbed relentlessly.

I remembered our encounter at Hamilton House when she had been unfaithful to Ernest, and then her apparent joy years later, knowing she was expecting another child.

Oh, look, Mother, Cal is walking now! He's taking his first step.

But most of all, I remembered the day the telegram came when she only wanted me, because she said only I could understand her grief over Stephen's death.

My God, Mama, they say Stephen is dead. It can't be true, can it? Tell them it can't be true. She called me "Mama" for the first time that day.

I remembered every emotion, every expression, and every heartbeat that this beloved daughter of mine had ever experienced. I also remembered that for much of her life I had been unable to fully share her joys and sorrows, because we were both too stubborn to understand and accept our differences.

In that one moment, her whole life flashed before my eyes, making me unbelievably sad and happy at the same time. I nodded to one of the seamen on duty.

"This is my daughter, Sarah McBride Hamilton," I said in a voice I barely recognized as my own. And then came that familiar darkness and I felt myself slipping to the ground, because suddenly everything was simply too much to bear.

I later learned that Teddy and Bertie had also identified Ernest. His casket was further down the row. We were more fortunate than many there that day. At least we would be able to bring our loved ones home to their final resting place.

CHAPTER 19

We held their funerals on November 15th. Cal insisted on going. He told me he wanted to send his mother and father to heaven to be with Stephen.

St. Luke's Church overflowed with those wanting to pay their respects to Sarah and Ernest. It was heart-warming to know so many people cared.

I was surprised by my own calm throughout the ceremony, even though inside I was hurting so unbearably. I was grateful most of all for Edward's support. This latest tragedy in our lives had aged him considerably, and he looked, for once, to be every one of his eighty-six years. Well, I was seventy-three myself, and on the day of my daughter's funeral, I felt my age.

After the ceremony, we adjourned to Providence with the family and some of our closest friends. A sombre air hung over us all. These were such unnecessary deaths, and Bertie told me on the side that investigations into the sinking of the *Princess Sophia* would most probably continue for many years.

"There will be many claims of negligence and so on. People are suing ..."

"For what?" I replied. "Suing won't bring them back."

"Maybe for Cal's sake, we should think about it, Mother. He has lost so much and should be entitled to compensation. I will take some advice from the Caldwells."

"Nothing, Bertie, can compensate him for the loss of his parents."

"Well, of course, not, Mother. I only meant—"

"I know, dear, you meant well by your remarks. Just look after the estate. Hamilton House will have to be sold and the money put in trust for Cal. That's all we need worry about for now."

"Yes, Mother."

I tried desperately hard to be pleasant and sociable to everyone. I was, as Gideon and Sarah would have said, playing the part of "the chatelaine of Providence." *Life must go on,* she was fond of telling me. The thought of hearing her say that to me made me smile momentarily, and as I looked up and across the room, I saw Letty standing in the doorway.

She rushed across the room and hugged me. "Oh, Granny Mac. You are being so brave," she said. "And poor little Cal. Is there anything I can do?"

"Letty, thank you dear. I am sure we can all help him get through this together."

She looked older than her twenty-one years. She must have witnessed so much tragedy and horror during the past four years as a nurse. Far too much for such a sweet, young girl, plus having lost the love of her life. And now, this!

"We are all trying to be strong for Cal, Letty. He has been so brave."

"Cal and I always got on so well. I will spend time with him, now as he has lost so much. Both his parents and his older brother."

"Thank you, dear. I would appreciate any help at all."

"Granny Mac, how would you feel about my moving permanently into Providence and helping you take care of him? I have already spoken with my parents, and even with Grandad, and they all think it would be the best thing now."

I smiled. "That's because they are worried that at my age I'm too old to take care of a young, lively boy. Even my two bachelor sons are getting up in age now, in their forties!"

"Oh, dear Granny Mac, you will never be too old to do anything you put your mind to, but I would love to do this for ... me, too. I feel that Stephen would want this, knowing his little brother has lost so much. And later, when you feel up to it, there is someone I would like you to meet. His name is Austin Harris, and he was one of the young men whose life Stephen saved before he died."

"My goodness ... how did you find him? Sarah and Ernest wanted to look for them—when they returned ..."

"He actually found us. He is in rehabilitation at Craigdarroch Castle Hospital right now, because he lost a leg. I think it would be a great comfort for you to talk to him."

"Thank you, dear. You must invite him to Providence later."

Letty nodded, and I noticed something in her expression which made me want to meet this young man. Yes, and it would be wonderful to have a pretty young face staying here with me again.

And so it was arranged. We became a motley group of people living at Providence. An old lady and her companion Dulcie, two middle-aged men set in their ways, a young girl whose life experiences had travelled far beyond her years, and who vowed to me the night of the funeral that she would never marry. And Cal, a lively lad whose life had been turned upside down so violently.

But I knew that somehow we would survive as long as we all had one another.

* * *

The day after the funeral, I picked up the mail from the silver tray in the hall myself and took it all into the library. Many of the letters were those of condolence, and I set them aside, determined to read them later when I was more able to cope.

But then I saw one postmarked from Juneau, in Sarah's distinctive handwriting. I knew immediately who had written it, and for a brief moment I forgot what had happened and foolishly imagined she was writing to tell me they would be home soon. My hand shook as I ripped open the envelope.

Darling Mama, it began. (I could not believe she had written "Mama" instead of Mother.)

Tonight I am unbelievably happy! Ernest and I have just returned from the Sour-Dough Ball—that's the North's best attempt at trying to be terribly formal! But, surprisingly, it was lots of fun, and Ernest and I enjoyed it immensely.

Guess what? We have decided to try for another baby. I know I am way past child-bearing years, but one never knows. As Ernest says, it will be fun trying.

You might think I sound terribly frivolous. That's probably because I am feeling so happy and at peace with my life tonight ... even about Stephen and everything. Tonight, at the ball, we ran into Etienne Dupont and his wife, a woman called Julia. Mama, I felt nothing! It was a wonderful relief, and I know now, for sure, that it is all safely in the past. He looked so much like Papa in many ways, not his colouring though. He, as you know, was much darker skinned and had black hair, but anyway I simply felt a 'sisterly' affection for him. Nothing more.

I truly love and appreciate Ernest with all my heart. I can't wait to see Cal again. Tell him ... oh, but we will probably be home before this letter reaches you, knowing how slow the mail can be ... but tell him anyway that we love him dearly and have missed him SO much.

Thank you, mama, for being the best of mothers. I am so sorry I have spent over forty years criticizing you and fighting with you over the silliest of things. What a waste of energy! Instead, I want you to know that I am so proud of you and I love you with all my heart. I ... I truly understand. Tonight, I feel like I have been given divine knowledge into all the secrets of life. Oh, how typically Sarah that sounds! SO dramatic. Maybe I should have become an actress after all!

I love you, dearest, and Ernest sends his love too. We will see you
around the 26th. The Princess Sophia sails on the 23rd, so it all depends on
what time we make and if the weather is good.

Your loving daughter,

Sarah.

I laughed and I cried as I clasped her letter close to my heart. I
wondered if perhaps she had already been pregnant when she died.
No point in thinking about that, though.

And then I mounted the stairs to my bedroom. From there I
slowly climbed up to the turret and opened the chest where I stored
all my journals. Between the pages for the year 1871, the year of Sarah's
birth, I carefully placed her letter.

Maybe one day, a long time from now, someone will read that
letter and know just how much we truly loved one another. But, for
now, it would remain between the two of us.

And then I walked over to the window, feeling a sudden peace
descending upon me. Outside, in the crisp November air, I saw Bertie
and Cal taking a walk down to the Arm, holding hands. My son and
my grandson.

Letty held his other hand, and I remembered what she had said
about meeting the young man whose life Stephen had saved. I looked
forward to that. I thought about Gideon and how he always said
providence led him to me and it was our destiny. Things happened
the way they are meant to, even though we don't always understand
the reason.

And in that moment, I am sure I heard Sarah's voice. *Cal is our*
future now, Mama. You have to remain strong for him.

She knew, just as I did, that the future of the McBride family now
rested on his small but very capable shoulders.

PART TWO

(1910–1941)

Flying High
CAL

"Carve your name on hearts, not tombstones. A legacy is etched into the minds of others and the stories they share about you."

Shannon Alder

CHAPTER 20

I was told that two auspicious events happened in Victoria on a September morning in 1910.

One occurred in a field near Mount Tolmie, where an adventurous chap by the name of William Wallace Gibson attempted to get off the ground and fly in his homemade "twin plane." The twin plane was a contraption he had built in the back yard of his James Bay home. Powered by an amateurish, homemade engine, Gibson's aircraft made a successful flight of 200 feet, just twenty feet above ground level, before promptly crashing into a tree. As a result, Gibson became the object of much ridicule, but in point of fact his brave attempt at flying was a remarkable achievement in Western Canada's aviation history

At approximately that same moment across town, my mother, Sarah Anne McBride Hamilton, was delivering me into the world in the master bedroom of Providence. All children in the McBride and Hamilton families had to be born at Providence, the McBride home.

Knowing my mother and the extremely gregarious woman that she was, I am sure she was putting on a first-class display of screaming and shrieking to herald my safe arrival. By saying that, I do not mean in any way to demean the hardships of childbearing. I merely want to emphasize that my mother was a fiery lady of spirit, and I am sure that, like everything else she did in life, she delivered me with gusto.

I mention these two events together because I feel it was a matter of particular irony that I was born at precisely the same moment that aviation history was being made in that Lansdowne field near Mount Tolmie in Victoria. In view of the way my life turned out, the two events happening simultaneously make it more than a little coincidental.

I remember very little of the first eight years of my life. I do recall images, most of which were happy. The precise events of the tragedy that occurred when I was eight seem thankfully to have been obliterated from my memory.

However, I do vividly remember my first home, Hamilton House, and I know we had a very large garden and a couple of boisterous dogs. I also remember I once had a much older brother who called us "The Happy Hamiltons." He then went off to fight in the Great War and never came back. They told me he was a hero because he had saved the lives of other men and sacrificed himself on the battle field. I recall thinking that he did not have to go so far away to prove he was a hero, because to me he already was one long before he left.

He and his girlfriend, Letty Caldwell, who lived next door to us, played with me a lot, especially out at Sooke Lake, where we owned a summer cabin. I remember that my mother was extremely beautiful and had a very infectious laugh, and I still recall the scent of her exotic perfume whenever she hugged me. Pops was quieter by nature, but he had a good sense of humour

Most of all, I remember moving to Providence to live with my grandmother and my two uncles because my parents had gone north for a holiday. I love Providence. It is a beautiful house and it sits right by the Gorge Arm, where I first learned to swim.

After that, the memories become a little blurry. Just images and sounds again, but most were not happy ones, so I must have decided to forget them. From somewhere in the distance, however, I can still hear the sound of bagpipes on Armistice Day, or was that at someone's funeral? Granny Mac told me that Mumsy and Pops had been drowned at sea in a terrible storm, so I would be staying with her now at Providence. We had to bury them up at St. Luke's Church, so maybe it was their funeral I remember.

I just know that suddenly everything seemed pretty grim. At night, when it was dark and I was supposed to be asleep, I would often start screaming because of those awful nightmares I kept having, but someone in the house always came running into my bedroom to calm me. Mostly it was Granny Mac, Uncle Bertie or Uncle Teddy, but whoever came would always hold me tight and comfort me through the long night.

I hated those nightmares, because they were always about drowning at sea, so I vowed I would never sail anywhere, and I was determined to be a strong swimmer.

Maybe I'd be much safer up in the air.

* * *

Eventually Letty also came to live with us, and things got much better. She was very kind to me and helped my grandmother take care of me. I began to forget most of the bad things that had happened to me, and the nightmares went away. That was good, because such tragedies are far too great for a child to bear. But I always kept a photograph of my mother and father beside my bed, and also one of my brother Steve, the war hero, so that I would never forget any of them. As time passed, the memory of their actual faces grew dim, so I looked at their photographs often.

Letty was like my big sister or my mother, and Uncle Bertie became a father figure. Letty had a friend called Austin Harris who had also been injured in the Great War, and he often visited us at Providence because I think he was courting Letty, although I wasn't really sure.

One day I plucked up the courage to ask him about his missing leg, because I was intrigued by his artificial one.

"Mr. Harris," I began, "what happened to your real leg?"

Granny Mac was shocked. "That is very rude, Caleb. Those are not the kind of questions you ask, young man," she said.

But Mr. Harris just smiled at me. "That's okay, Caleb. Naturally, you are curious. Well, I left it somewhere in France."

"But why did you leave it there? Didn't you want it anymore?"

He laughed. "Oh yes, I wanted it very much, but I had a battle with an explosive, and I lost the battle and my leg was badly injured, so I had to have it amputated."

"That means cut off, right? That must have been very painful."

"Yes, it was a bit, but it's all right now, and I like my new wooden one. Your big brother, Stephen, saved my life that day, so I'm grateful for having one good leg left."

I noticed Letty placed her hand over his, and I wondered if she would ever marry him, because I felt sure he must have asked her. But she had loved my brother very much, and they were once engaged. I decided I wouldn't mind if she did marry Austin, though, because I think he made her happy and I rather liked him. It would be all right if he lived here with her, but if it meant she would move away, I didn't think I wanted that.

Uncle Teddy also lived with us. He was a doctor and he looked after me with the greatest of care whenever I was sick. Best of all, I had Granny Mac. She was my rock and my best friend. I loved talking to her and telling her about my dreams for the future. Although I knew she did not approve of what she called "those beastly flying machines," she at least listened to me and seemed interested, and never once did she discard my dreams as being unrealistic.

"I read something that Leonardo da Vinci said about flying, Granny Mac," I told her one day.

"Really, and what was that?"

"He said, '*I have always felt it is my destiny to build a machine that would allow man to fly.*'"

"Goodness me, where did you read that?"

"In one of your books about all the great artists, Granny Mac."

"How fascinating! Your reading skills are excellent. And to be able to remember a quote like that is quite exceptional. I'm proud of you, Caleb."

She seemed more proud of the fact that I could read so well than she did about the fact that someone like Leonardo da Vinci had seen the future of flying so long ago.

However, she did allow Uncle Bertie to take me to air shows. I remember the first time we went to one at Willows Camp, over in Oak Bay. It was in July of 1919, and I was almost nine. The Great War was now behind us, and people were trying desperately to think positively and be happy again. A great number of airmen had returned safely from the war and were eager to convince the government that there was potential in the field of aviation for the future. The Aerial League of Canada had been formed to promote aviation, and various air shows were held across the country.

The one at Willows Camp that year was great fun. We actually saw some formation flying and dog fights using Curtiss JN-4 Jenny trainers. A number of these "Jennies" were for sale at the end of the war for a few hundred dollars, and I begged Uncle Bertie to buy one. He didn't agree, but, on the other hand, he didn't turn down the idea altogether. He just said his favourite phrase: "We shall see in a few years." A person had to be at least eighteen to fly one anyway, and I was only nine.

That same summer, Granny's housekeeper and chauffeur, the Stapletons, announced they were returning to New York, where they had been offered very prestigious positions with a member of the wealthy Rockefeller family. Granny Mac was very annoyed about this and thought they were being very 'uppity.' She now only had one maid and Dulcie as her companion, plus a couple of Chinese men who worked in the gardens, so she advertised for another couple to come and work at Providence. The days of the typical "housekeeper and butler" were fast coming to an end, however, and such couples were becoming a rarity.

A couple named Arthur and Nell Potter applied for the job and, with their excellent references, Granny Mac hired them on the spot.

They had just arrived from Britain and both spoke with a strange cockney accent.

"Their accents grate on my nerves," Granny Mac repeatedly said, but she tolerated it because they were such good workers and they were the best help she had had around Providence since the departure of her beloved Ah Foo so many years ago, long before I was born.

The Potters did indeed work hard, and I particularly liked Arthur Potter because he could tinker with car engines and seemed to know a great deal about the mechanics of all engines, even those in airplanes. He never minded when I went down to the carriage house, which was now called the garage, and asked him a lot of questions.

By the time I was ten, I was an avid reader, and I had learned through reading that the Jennies I had seen in air shows were now transporting mail on long-distance flights. I frequently talked to Uncle Bertie about them.

"Perhaps McBride's Transportation should get into the flying business, Uncle Bertie," I begged with boyish enthusiasm.

Eventually he agreed, and in June of 1921, McBride's purchased four of the Aerial League Jennies and soon won contracts to fly mail between Vancouver, Victoria and Nanaimo. As Uncle Bertie pointed out, we were once again diversifying the business by broadening our interests.

As for me, I was simply ecstatic because I was now certain what part I wanted to play in the McBride family business.

CHAPTER 21

Meanwhile I had to survive my school years, and *survival* was the operative word.

Granny Mac and both my uncles all agreed that I was smart if I put my mind to it, so before entering the family business, they wanted me to attend university. McGill was one option, and the other was Oxford in England. The trouble was that I did not always put my mind to school work and barely managed to scrape through each year until graduation. There had been far too many distractions along the way, most of them of the female kind.

As I approached my seventeenth birthday in the summer of 1927, my two uncles must have decided unanimously that it was high time they gave me a lecture on sex, because it was apparent even to them that my interest in girls was becoming somewhat excessive. I would soon be going off to university and would need to know the ways of the world.

Usually, every evening the uncles occupied their own respective armchair on either side of the fireplace in the drawing room, but on that particular evening only Uncle Bertie was sitting there when I bounded in after a game of football, a sport that was quickly becoming very popular in Victoria.

"Ah, Caleb my boy," said Uncle Bertie, puffing on his pipe. "Can you spare a moment, old chap?"

I figured that he must have something pretty important on his mind, because he was actually smoking in a forbidden place. Granny Mac only allowed smoking in the library, which the uncles now called their den.

"Sure, Uncle B. What's up?"

He looked at me a little disapprovingly. Like my grandmother, he did not approve of my Canadianized expressions or my accent.

"It has come to our attention that you are associating with a number of young ladies of a ... well, slightly lower class, and not altogether the type with whom you should be mixing. Your grandmother is concerned, old boy, and wanted me to give you a bit of a lecture on, well, you know, how to conduct yourself, so to speak ... if you get yourself into a situation."

A situation! Ye gods, this was going to be good.

I sat down and waited, trying not to laugh. I knew Uncle Bertie had a reputation himself with the ladies, so I wondered how on earth he would go about trying to dissuade me from the same path he had undoubtedly taken.

"Have to be darned careful, old chap," he began.

"In what way, Uncle B?"

"Well, don't get yourself into a mess with a girl." He cleared his throat. "You know what I mean, eh?"

"No, Uncle B," I replied innocently. "What kind of a mess?" I enjoyed making him squirm. This was fun.

"Well, you know ... get her in the family way. Preggers. You know about that stuff, don't you, old chap? How it all works and so on."

"Not really, Uncle B," I replied innocently. I wanted to hear his version anyway.

"Oh, well, I'll get your Uncle Teddy to explain the mechanics of it. After all, he's a doctor. And, when you're a bit older, say eighteen, I'll take you myself to one of the clubs in town. Young men naturally have to let off steam once in a while of course."

"Oh, of course," I replied dutifully.

He then went on to ask about my game, so I assume his attempt at introducing me to sex and enlightening me about the evils of the wrong type of woman was over.

I knew that Uncle Bertie had once been married, but now no one ever mentioned the notorious Antoinette, who had supposedly run off to Australia with another man. On one occasion, I had overheard Granny Mac saying that "it was good riddance to bad rubbish."

The next night, obviously by prearrangement, it was Uncle Teddy's turn. He called me into the library after dinner, asked me to sit down and then approached the whole matter from a completely different angle. He assumed that I was in a virginal state of complete ignorance, so he had come armed with illustrated anatomy books, which I found very explicit and rather exciting. Certainly the pictures were incredible.

He also talked of love and commitment and treating women with the greatest of respect. He only briefly touched on my "letting off steam," before, undoubtedly, I would find a delightfully pure young lady with whom I would spend the rest of my life in marital bliss.

Uncle Teddy had also been married. His wife had been Margaret Bowers, my mother's best friend, and I knew she had died young and that Uncle Teddy had loved her so much that he had never remarried.

I adored my two uncles, and I was grateful for their joint, but utterly diverse, points of view on the mysteries of the female sex. What neither of them knew was that I had already lost my virginity three months earlier.

Thinking back to those two evenings and my uncles' embarrassed attempts at helping me become a man, I am grateful to them both, for, from their totally different viewpoints about women and sexual relationships, they somehow managed to present to me the best of both worlds.

* * *

The occasion of my lost virginity three months earlier had not exactly been a resounding success, but it was a starting point and gave me an appetite for more of the same.

Her name was Serena, and she was the older sister of a school chum named Charlie Fuller. Charlie was not the sort of friend with whom my family would have wanted me to associate. He lived in a rough area of town with his single mother and older sister. He told me his father had run off and left them years ago, and he wasn't even sure whether his parents had actually ever been married. His scandalous history rather intrigued me, plus he had a great sense of humour, and we got along very well.

Actually, he was quite a bright chap, because he had won a scholarship to our all-boys school. Certainly his mother would never have been able to afford the fees. I'm not sure exactly how she made money to support her family, although she called herself a seamstress, and I loved going to their house because it was relaxed and very bohemian. Everything was casual and no one "kept up appearances" like we did at Providence. No one dressed for dinner or said grace before we ate. No one "retired to the drawing room" to drink tea or coffee, or smoked cigars in the den only, mainly because there wasn't a den anyway. And no one told a sweet old uncle to put out his pipe in the drawing room because of its foul smell.

Only at Providence did we have to listen to classical music, mostly Beethoven or Mozart, played by my grandmother on her grand piano. Although I loved listening to her play and actually enjoyed playing myself, I never dared play any of the popular music of the day while Granny Mac was at home. I only did that when I was alone. I loved my grandmother dearly, but she did have some rather strict, old-fashioned rules.

By contrast, there were no rules at Charlie Fuller's house. I especially liked his mother and sister, because they were both so worldly and wore outrageously colourful clothes with skirts that were extremely short. They had an old phonograph machine in their parlour which we had to wind up before we could play records. We then jigged around the room to popular tunes such as "Crazy Rhythm," "Black

Bottom," "My Blue Heaven" or "Yes, We Have No Bananas." Even
Charlie's mother joined in.

I had assumed Serena was about eighteen, and it was only after
our sexual encounter that I learned she was actually a very experienced
twenty-one-year-old, who had most probably delighted in deflowering
a young man of sixteen.

The decade of the '20s had earned itself the title "the roaring
twenties," and I could quite see why. After the gloom and sadness
of the war years, the world needed fun and gaiety, and, as I passed
through my teen years, I was more than ready to be a part of it all and
to contribute as much as I could.

With what little finances her family had, Serena tried to emulate
the typical 1920s woman known as the flapper. She smoked, she drank,
and, whenever possible, she danced the night away. Her hair was cut
short, often hidden by a brightly coloured cloche hat, and she wore
oodles of makeup and went to as many parties as she could. To me,
her scarlet lips, her long rows of beads, her short, fringed skirt and
her giddy disposition were all that I needed to enter into manhood.

But there was no doubt about it; Serena was a nymphomaniac,
or, as some called such young ladies, a "charity girl." Charity begins at
home, so they say, and that is where it began for Serena and me, in her
home one afternoon when we were alone. Between us, we consumed
a few glasses of bootlegged whisky, the effects of which made me as
giddy as she was. Nothing stopped Serena from doing anything . She
was insatiable.

Our "affair," if it could be called that, lasted two months. By then
she was bored with me and I was totally exhausted. By that time, I had
also discovered her true age and felt some guilt about that, although
I have no idea why. Instead, I should have been rather proud of my
abilities to satisfy an older woman, if only briefly.

Eventually she moved on to greener pastures. A producer from
Hollywood arrived in town, and Serena decided she wanted to be an

actress. The next thing we knew, she had left for California with this guy and with the blessing of her mother, who forever after referred to her daughter as "the movie star." I never saw Serena again, even though Charlie occasionally told me about a small part she had in a movie.

As for me, I moved on to a period of celibacy. Needless to say, after my experiences with Serena, it was destined to be short.

* * *

By the beginning of 1928, a decision had been made about my future. My final grades had miraculously allowed me to enter Oxford University in England the following September. My grandmother, uncles and Letty were ecstatic.

Meanwhile, Uncle Bertie appreciated my frequent, enthusiastic input into the family business, especially the new McBride's Airways division. On January 1st 1928, B.C. Airways opened up its first airport at Lansdowne Field, the same field where Gibson had made his maiden flight eighteen years earlier.

Since turning fifteen, I had been allowed to take short flights in our own McBride's aircraft and had once flown in an Alexander Eagle Rock plane from Lansdowne Airport, piloted by a fellow called Wilson. I had eventually even persuaded my grandmother to allow me to take lessons at the flying school there. She reluctantly agreed to this because she probably figured it was safer to have me learn the finer points of flying from experts, rather than make a foolhardy attempt to fly on my own.

In July of 1928, two months before I was due to leave for university, a BC Airways trimotor G-CATX 'plane arrived at Lansdowne. Many Victoria politicians and notables headed out to the airport to have their photograph taken with the plane. The McBrides and Caldwells were, of course, present that day, including Great Uncle Edward Caldwell, now ninety-six, walking upright with the aid of his cane. On August 16, the Trimotor began its scheduled passenger flights between Victoria and Seattle. But tragedy struck just a few days later, when we learned that the Trimotor had crashed into the sea near Port Townsend in Washington.

"This will hopefully put an end to flying," Granny Mac said when we received the news. "Cal, it is far too dangerous. Man was not meant to be up there in the air. It is completely unnatural."

"Granny," I said, taking her small hand in mine. "Every new invention throughout history was thought to be unnatural. And sometimes people have to be sacrificed for the greater good, because initially mistakes will be made. But we *will* get it right, and one day, flying will be a perfectly safe and acceptable means of travel."

"Never!" she replied, adamantly. "Never!"

But something far more important occupied all our thoughts at the end of that month. Great Uncle Edward Caldwell became desperately ill with pneumonia. Until a few weeks before, he had still been taking his "daily constitution," walking from his house in James Bay into downtown Victoria, or over to Providence to visit with my grandmother. But then he caught a bad chill that turned to pneumonia, and he peacefully passed away on September 1.

It was the day I was supposed to leave by train on the first stage of my journey to Oxford. However, I wanted to be with my grandmother and comfort her in her sorrow for her long-time friend, so I decided to put off my departure.

It was the most incredible affair. Hundreds of the town's citizens turned out to honour this man, who, like my grandfather McBride, had pioneered the lifestyle we now enjoyed in Victoria. He was so greatly respected and so honourably eulogized at St. Luke's that day that I doubt there was a dry eye in the place.

Many of us were called upon to speak at the service, and all our words were of great appreciation for all that he had achieved in his long lifetime. His son James, himself now in his seventies, spoke with deep emotion of the father he had loved and respected. His grandsons Joe, with his wife, Emily, and Kit and his wife Laura from Dawson City, were present to honour him. His granddaughter Anna, and her family in England, sent messages to be read in their absence. His great-grandchildren, including Letty, William and John, mourned his loss, as did we, the McBrides, lesser in number but equal in love.

My grandmother had asked me to read something on behalf of the McBride family. I felt honoured that she had asked me rather than Uncle Bertie or Uncle Teddy. As I walked to the front of the church to deliver my words, I looked back at Granny Mac, her head bowed and covered in black crepe, her tiny hands clasped tightly, and her small shoulders heaving with emotion as she took deep breaths to try to dispel the tears she undoubtedly would later cry. She was eighty-five years old herself, but her tiny frame and her relatively unlined features, now hidden beneath yards of black cloth, had always made her seem twenty years younger.

I knew she had lost so much in her lifetime. Her beloved husband, her daughter, and long ago, a small son after whom I had been named. And, now, she had lost her dearest and oldest friend. I wondered how I would manage to get through my speech without breaking down. But I did, for her sake.

As I walked back to my seat, she raised her head slightly, nodding her approval. I think she mouthed the words "well done," and I felt proud that I had been able to do this man justice on her behalf.

CHAPTER 22

Charlie had plans to attend university in Toronto—in fact, we'd hoped to travel that far together on our way to this new adventure—but he'd explained that he really wanted to work and earn some money first. So, wanting to keep Granny Mac company while she felt so low, I also decided to delay my start at Oxford until we could head off together. Much to Uncle Bertie's delight, I worked in the family business for a while. He even agreed to hire Charlie.

So it wasn't until I turned twenty-one in September of 1931 that Charlie and I finally began our journey east, but by then my heart was no longer in pursuing education.

North America was suffering under a depression that was hitting the entire continent with a vengeance. There were signs all around us, and, for the first time in my life, I felt guilty for being one of the wealthy.

McBride's Transportation would undoubtedly suffer also as a result of a depressed economy, but not to any great degree. People like the McBrides, the Hamiltons, and the Caldwells would not be on the streets looking for handouts, riding the rails to somewhere else, or lining up at soup kitchens for a hot meal.

To my way of thinking, it somehow seemed wrong for a rich kid like me to be heading off to Oxford to enjoy four years of education when all around me people were struggling to simply survive.

Charlie Fuller, on the other hand, had only known poverty in his lifetime, and he was excited about the prospect of finally gaining an education that would allow him to step up in the world. I could understand his point of view, but I could not rid myself of those feelings of despair for all the less fortunate.

We only got as far as Vancouver. Before boarding the train for the east, we had a night on the town visiting some clubs, and at one of them that had just opened, called the Railway Club, we happened to meet up with a chap named Les Gordon, who was a well-known pilot in British Columbia at that time.

"Did you guys know that 'barnstorming' is fast becoming a popular way to make a living for anyone in the aviation business? Pilots are flying around the province, stopping off at various towns and enticing people to go for a ride in their planes for a small fee," he told us. And apparently every time they set up their aircraft in fields near a barn (hence the adopted term), they attracted large crowds.

"It doesn't pay much, because most people don't have the money to spare these days, but it covers the cost of gas plus a bit extra, and it's a way to make an honest buck," he added with a grin. "It also helps out the farmers when we rent their fields. They need all the extra money they can get these days." We both nodded our agreement.

"How come you young fellows are so interested in flying?" I guess he wondered because I had been asking him a million questions.

"Well, I'm crazy about it, always have been," I said. "I've taken flying lessons over on the Island and flown solo a few times from Lansdowne. I'm off to university now, but I sure would prefer to be doing what you're describing."

"When do you start at university?" he asked.

"I have to be in England by the end of September, when I start at Oxford."

"Oxford, eh? You must be a smart kid." *And a rich one,* he was probably thinking.

I grinned. "Not really. I just got lucky with my grades. Charlie here, he's the smart one. He's off to the University of Toronto."

"Wow, two smart-asses! Well, Hamilton, you seem to know a helluva lot about flying, and I sure could use a guy like you. Pity you have to head off to England right now."

"Use a guy like me? In what way?"

I could see Charlie shaking his head and I knew what he was thinking. He figured I was about to get him roped into something outrageous, which I had been wont to do on many an occasion in the past.

"Well, I have a couple of two-seater planes sitting in a field two miles from here," replied Les. "Right now, I'm renting the field from a farmer and have been taking people up for rides and making a bit of money, but I really need a second pilot so that both planes can operate at the same time. That way, I'll double the profits. I also need someone on the ground to organize things, someone with a good business head."

A light flashed on in my head at that moment, and I knew it had been fate that I had run into Les Gordon on that particular night. Oxford could wait. Right now I wanted to fly. I didn't need the money for myself, but maybe I could help others who were suffering through these depression times. And I also needed the flying experience.

Suddenly, I knew exactly what I wanted to do. The only trouble was, how would I convince my uncles and my grandmother—and, more importantly at that precise moment, Charlie, who was still hell bent on heading for Toronto to begin his studies.

"Look, Les," I hesitated for a moment. "I could perhaps put off university for a bit and ..."

Charlie spluttered into his beer. "Put off university? Are you mad, Mac?"

"Well, think about it, man. We're only twenty-one. We've got years ahead of us. Why not try something else for a while, before going to university?"

"Oh yeah ... and I'd like to hear you explain that logic to your grandmother."

"I can convince her, don't worry," I replied with all the bravado of the young. I turned to Les, who was studying us both with great interest. "Could you excuse us for a moment, Les?" I said. "I'd like to talk to Charlie alone for a moment."

"Sure, sure," he replied, removing himself and his beer away from the bar where we were all seated.

"Now, Charlie," I lowered my voice. "Listen to me. This is a great opportunity for us both. You, with your brains and organizational skills, could be the man on the ground at the business end. And with me up in the air with my flying experience, how can we go wrong?"

He laughed. "Flying experience? Mac, you've only had a few lessons over at Lansdowne. And how many times, for God's sake, have you flown solo?"

"Enough, Charlie. I'm good, and I know it. I could do this."

"And what about me? What makes you think I want to be the brains behind this hair- brained scheme? I *need* an education, Mac, and I won that scholarship through blood, sweat and tears. I sure intend to use it now."

"You can, Charlie—in a year. But for now, this is a great opportunity for us to see life. And another thing, don't call me Mac."

"Why? I've always called you that, never Cal or Caleb, like the rest of your family."

"Yeah, because of my middle name, McBride. But I don't want Les Gibson knowing I have any connection to the McBrides or to McBride's Transportation; otherwise he'll wonder what the heck I'm doing this for."

"He's not the only one!"

I ignored his pessimism. "He'll also think I want to invest money in his business, which I don't. I just want to gain some more flying experience, and maybe, at the same time, we can help out in these hard times."

"Christ, Mac, you sound like a bloody do-gooder!"

"Well, why not, Charlie? All my life, I've had everything handed to me on a silver platter. Now, I want to give something back."

"I see your point, Mac, but that's your life, not mine. I don't even know what a silver platter looks like, for Christ's sake. Only education is going to give me the kind of lifestyle you've always known."

I thought about that for a moment. He was right. I had no right to include him in this. It was my dream, not his.

"Okay, Charlie. You win. You go ahead and get your education, but I'm staying here."

"Mac, think about it!"

"I'm done with thinking. This is what I want to do, but I can't expect you to fall in with it. That's unfair. You deserve your time at university, and you'll come back an educated academic twit in a few years, and I'll still be a fly-boy. But at least I have the family business to fall back on if I need it. You don't."

He laughed. "Maybe you won't, either, once you tell your grand-mother. She may cut you off!"

"True, but I'll be doing what I've wanted to do all my life, and maybe I'll compromise by telling her I'm just postponing Oxford for a year. Anyway, I'm in, so I'm telling Les right now."

"Hold on," Charlie grabbed my arm. "Just for a year, you say? Do you mean that?"

"Sure. It will just be a fun experience before I'm ready to settle down to studying."

He raised his eyes skyward in a gesture of hopelessness. "God help me, Mac, but I'm about to say and do something I hope I never live to regret."

"And what would that be, Charlie Fuller?"

"I'm about to tell you that I'm 'in' too. Let's break the news to this guy before I change my mind."

I thumped him on the back. "You won't regret this, Charlie, I promise."

"I already do," he replied. "But just for a year, though, eh?"

"Just for a year," I promised.

CHAPTER 23

Les Gordon was delighted we had both agreed to join him.

"But lad, I thought you said your name was Cal Hamilton. Why does your buddy call you Mac?"

"It's his middle name," interjected Charlie. "Caleb McBride Hamilton. Too much of a mouthful, don't you think? So I've always called him just plain Mac."

"Sounds good to me. Then just plain Mac it is." From that moment on, I was always known in the aviation business as Mac Hamilton.

I winked at Charlie and we called for another round. The next morning, with a hangover second to none, I put in a phone call to Providence.

"You've done *what*?" screeched my grandmother over the static on the line.

"I've become a pilot, a barnstormer. Charlie and I have decided to join forces with Les Gordon. You must have heard of him, Granny Mac. He's a well-known pilot in British Columbia. He's running a small operation up and down the Fraser River right now, and I'm going to be his second pilot. Charlie's doing the business stuff."

"And would you mind telling me why you are not on the train heading for Oxford instead?"

"I've just told you, Gran. I've postponed it—but only for a year."

"I am speechless, Cal. Just speechless. You have thrown away a great opportunity. Why would you do such a crazy thing? This is pure madness, and so dangerous, too. I am handing you over to your Uncle Bertie. Maybe he can knock some sense into you."

"But Gran ..."

She was gone and then Uncle Bertie's voice came bellowing down through the static. "Young man, I cannot believe what I'm hearing," he said. "Is it true you have decided to take up flying?"

"Yes, Uncle Bertie. I'm barnstorming for a while."

"You're *what*?"

"I'm taking people up for rides in one of Les Gordon's two-seater planes."

"Goodness, Cal, you could have stayed in Victoria and worked for McBride's Aviation if you wanted to fly that much. We're using pilots to transport mail all over the island, as you well know, but we had such faith in your abilities and felt you would do so well at Oxford. Why would you want to forfeit all of that, for goodness' sake?"

"I'm not forfeiting it, Uncle Bertie. I'm just postponing it, and I'm sure that you and Granny can fix it with the dean. Just give me a year on my own. One short year, and I promise I'll head off to academia after that. And then I'll return and take up the helm at McBride's, I promise."

"Letty is going over to Vancouver to talk to you tomorrow. Maybe she can change your mind. You've really put the wind up our sails, young man."

"I know, Uncle B, and I'm truly sorry, but please understand, this is what I really have to do right now. Please put Granny back on the line."

More crackles and then Granny Mac's voice. "So, I see you are as headstrong as your mother always was," she said with a sigh.

"I guess so, Granny. I am sorry to worry and upset you, but I promise it is for the best. You'll see. I'll be a famous pilot one day, and this will give me all the experience I need. And I'm not doing it for the money, Gran. It seems wrong that there are so many people going without these days. The streets over here are full of begging people with no food, no jobs, and no future to look forward to. Maybe I can help with my own money. Money *I* will have made myself ..."

"Oh, Cal," she said. I thought for a moment that she might be crying. Her voice suddenly went quiet and a little shaky. "You sound so much like your mother, Cal. Whatever will I do with you? Just, please stay safe."

"I will Gran, I promise."

As long as I had her blessing, I thought I was invincible.

* * *

Charlie and I met Letty in Ladner, and she came out to the field with us to inspect the two aeroplanes. Les Gordon seemed immediately attracted to her, but I felt he was wasting his time. Letty was now almost thirty and since Steve's death had shown absolutely no interest in any man other than her friend Austin, but nothing seemed to have come of that.

Although she had obviously been sent by the family on a mission in a last-ditch attempt to change my mind, we somehow managed to get her as enthusiastic about barnstorming as we had become. Even Charlie was no longer a passive bystander in the operation. It had suddenly become a great adventure for us all.

Letty returned to Victoria with a promise to assure Granny Mac and the uncles that what we were doing was perfectly safe and would be a great life experience for us all. I have no idea how we managed to convince her of that, but I think secretly she rather envied our spirit and *joie de vivre*. After all, hadn't she and my brother Steve been equally adventurous when they took off for Europe in the Great War?

It was amazing that so many people wanted to take a ride in a plane, even in times of economic depression. Everyone seemed to look at flying as a means of escape, an incredible adventure away from all their worries. Every day, people came out in droves to line up for the thrill of a lifetime—men, women, young children and even their dogs. Each person was weighed in by Charlie and then was charged a fare according to their poundage. We particularly liked to find as many overweight people as possible, as we were charging by the pound. For a ten-minute ride, a fare could cost as much as five dollars.

Needless to say, my own flying skills were put to the test in a big way, but Les Gordon was patient with any errors I made and was an excellent teacher. It did not take me long to prove my worth to him and learn a few tricks along the way.

It was, of course, a ridiculous madness that overwhelmed us all. The planes, two DH60X Cirrus Moths, were somewhat unreliable at best. Flying at reasonably low altitudes, where we could spot familiar landmarks on the ground, was by far the safest way to go, because we only had road maps to guide us. We carried an extra gas tank underneath the plane, with a small box on the side in which we placed an axe, a few rations, and a revolver. Gordon insisted on this, especially when we flew further up the Fraser Canyon. He said that if at any time we had to land because of bad weather conditions, we might be stranded for some time. But quite honestly, as the country up the canyon was totally foreign to us all, we had no idea where we would have been able to land safely anyway in such terrain. Nonetheless, we soldiered on, taking our lives recklessly in our hands as though there was no tomorrow.

Weather was always a problem, because there were no weather reports to rely on, and a wind storm or dense fog could develop unexpectedly at any moment. Navigation was non-existent. As barnstormers, we learned to fly by instinct. Landmarks such as railroad tracks, roads, and especially power lines became our guidelines. Mountains, especially high ones, became our enemies.

We utilized the field in Ladner for as long as possible and came out of that episode with a thousand dollars apiece in our pockets, after paying the farmer his rental fee. Les Gordon then offered to make me a partner, because I think he had soon realized I was as crazy as he was. I was dubbed "Mac, the crazy comedian" in the partnership, because by then I had been putting on acrobatic shows over the field for some time. We had purchased an Eaglerock and taken on another pilot, Jack, and Charlie worked the office and looked after the business side of things.

People paid to come and see our air shows when the three of us flew in formation; then the leader plane would flip over and fly upside-down, with the other two flying right-side-up down the middle of the field, very low to the ground. I also did a solo act where I pretended to be crashing the plane but pulled out at the last minute. The dust would fly, the crowds would scream with delight, and then let out a collective sigh of relief as I righted the plane at the proverbial last moment and ascended again, thus avoiding disaster.

I knew that I was a complete idiot, and each time I climbed into the cockpit I realized it might be for the last time. It was a sort of fatalistic theory. What was to be was meant to be. I was playing a dangerous game and a stupid one, but I was young, and the thrill of flying was addictive. Once in the sky, I felt completely at home, almost godlike. I knew then how my grandfather must have felt on the ocean. Aside from all the daredevil acrobatics and craziness, there was a kind of peace and wonderment about being high above the earth, flying through clouds and being close to the sun and the sky. Flying was quite simply entrenched in my blood.

Later we all left for Merritt in the interior, where we set up our business once again. Again, we were treated like conquering heroes, especially by the women, who seemed to be totally enthralled by our lifestyle and the strange clothes we wore: the breeches, the big boots and the leather jackets, always of course with a gaily coloured scarf flung in wild abandon around our necks. Helmets and goggles completed the ensemble.

Everywhere we went, we were entertained royally, wined and dined by officials or in the homes of private citizens, and there was never a shortage of women who were all more than willing to show us their appreciation for the thrills we gave the crowds in the sky. They seemed to think it their honour-bound duty to return the favour with equal thrills on the ground. And who were we to object?

It continued to amaze me that the crowds still kept coming out to see us put on a show, or to go up with us for a ten-minute joy ride. Sometimes we made as much as five hundred dollars a day. But I kept my promise. After taking a small amount of my share for everyday living expenses, I gave most of it away to the charities, soup kitchens and a few relief camps throughout the province. It gave me a great deal of satisfaction to know that I was finally giving something back after a lifetime of living the good life. I had seen far too much poverty by then—constantly witnessing desperate men riding the rails to God-knows-where in an attempt to find work.

CHAPTER 24

In September of 1932, Charlie left for Toronto, and this time I did not try to stop him. He had stayed for far longer than originally planned, partly because he was enjoying himself immensely, but mostly out of loyalty to me.

"Mac, you've got to give up this craziness eventually too, you know," he said with a grin. "Education is important, and we've already had a good run at this nonsense and made some money."

"I know, old chap, I know. But *this* is what I want to do with my life."

"Well, you could still be a pilot, but at least you'd be an educated one!"

"So right now, I'm just a blithering idiot, is that what you're telling me?"

"You said it, not me!" He laughed. We had our last beer together as we wished each other well. That night, he caught the train for Toronto. He had learned a few things about flying himself and had even handled a plane as my co-pilot on occasion, so I had a sneaking suspicion we would cross paths again in the world of aviation.

Soon after Charlie left, Les, Jack and I started our own flying school, training young men as pilots for the future. I still put on the air shows as well, doing my crazy flying stunts, but as I neared twenty-two in 1932 I was rather enjoying the business of passing on my skills to others. Soon we had one school in Ladner and another back on Vancouver Island near Duncan.

Whenever I was over on the Island, I stayed at Providence with Granny Mac, and she seemed to relish my visits and never once pressured me about Oxford. I knew I had broken my promise to her, but I think she could see how happy I was. I loved to tell her the outrageous tales of my flying escapades and make her laugh or screech with horror as I exaggerated each terrifying moment.

"I cannot believe you come from my blood, Cal! You are totally impossible!" she told me on more than one occasion, but always with a smile on her face.

And she never told me to stop. Actually, it was another person on one of my earlier visits back to the island who had really made me think again about the importance of an education and rethink my course in life.

It was ironic that he also just happened to be the most famous flyer in the world at that time. His name was Charles Augustus Lindbergh.

* * *

The day Charles Lindbergh came to Victoria was one few Victorians would ever forget.

Following another world tour, Lindbergh was due to arrive aboard the liner the *President Jefferson* on the evening of October 21, 1931, but his arrival was delayed because of fierce storms off the west coast. I was in Victoria at the time on an earlier visit to Providence and most of the town's citizens had woken early the following morning, having heard the liner was now due to dock around 4 a.m. It was a crisp autumn morning as the crowd began to gather at the Outer Wharf. Les, Jack and I had been invited, along with a number of other aviators, to be part of the welcoming committee, which also included the United States consul, Victoria's Mayor Herbert Anscomb, and many other dignitaries.

We all knew of Lindbergh's many achievements, which were by then legendary. Although still only a young man of twenty-nine, he had flown his monoplane *The Spirit of St. Louis* in record time from San Diego, California, to New York in 1927. On May 20th of that same year he had continued his flight alone across the Atlantic to Paris, arriving on the evening of the 21st after a non-stop flight of 3,610 miles in 33.5 hours.

In France and throughout Europe, he had been wined and dined by presidents, kings and princes, and upon arrival back in the States, President Herbert Hoover had received him at the White House. He had even been treated to a ticker-tape parade through the streets of New York and had become adored and revered around the world, by everyone from the ordinary man on the street to flying enthusiasts.

His arrival in Victoria that day was part of yet another world tour, and it was now Victoria's turn to honour him, though his appearance would be brief. The welcoming committee greeted him at the dock and drove him out to Lansdowne Airport. There a Lockheed Vega monoplane, which could attain a speed of one hundred and ninety miles per hour, awaited him, and his party and would carry them away to Seattle on the last lap of their journey home.

The first impression I had of my all-time hero was of a shy young man, with unruly blond, wavy hair. He was extremely tall and thin and, at first glance, it seemed difficult to believe he could have achieved so much. He was the epitome of the ordinary man, not at all how one would imagine a hero to look.

At Lansdowne Airport, Lindbergh made the customary speech in a reserved and reticent manner, but when a reporter asked him his views concerning Victoria's future position in aviation, his reply was both strong and adamant.

"I think Victoria should have an adequate airport, as, being the nearest point to the Orient, it will play a strategic part in the future of aviation. Aviation is the coming thing, and we must all accept that."

Another reporter then asked Mrs. Lindbergh about her son, Charles Junior. "When we left home he was just starting to walk," she said, smiling. "We can't wait to get back to him."

Her reply was also cheered loudly, and then a number of us in the group were individually introduced to Lindbergh and his wife, Anne.

When he shook my hand, he said: "Mac Hamilton? I've heard of you. You're that crazy barnstormer, aren't you?"

"Guilty, I'm afraid," I replied, hardly believing that he had actually heard of me.

"Well, I did the same thing myself a few years ago. Then I decided to get a bit of education, so I went off to Wisconsin University and studied mechanics. Never regretted it."

"Really?"

"Every bit of education you get in life, old chap, helps you in some way."

And then he passed on to the next man in the line, leaving me in awe that I had actually shaken the hand of the great Charles Lindbergh.

His plane had to be manually manoeuvred into position for take-off, and Lindbergh himself supervised us as we all helped move the machine. The crowds continued to cheer and clap.

With Lindbergh himself at the controls, the plane was finally ready for take-off. It rose swiftly to a height of about a thousand feet and eventually disappeared from view. The crowds slowly dispersed, but we were still all talking excitedly about the Lindberghs, reluctant to let go of that magical moment in time when a real live hero had graced us with his presence.

That night, over dinner at Providence, I told Granny Mac, Letty and my two uncles that I would soon be ready to take up my studies in Oxford and would like to start with the September 1934 semester if it could be arranged. Before that. I would dissolve my business with Les after we finished all our commitments in 1932 and 1933. I was through with barnstorming and ready for the next stage in my life. Everyone of course, was delighted with my decision, and they all drank to my health and future success in the land of academia.

Less than six months after that auspicious meeting with Lindbergh, the whole world was rocked by the news that the Lindberghs' young son had been kidnapped. A ransom of fifty thousand dollars was paid for his safe return, but tragically the child was found dead in May and Bruno Richard Hauptmann was arrested for the crime and brought to trial.

I shuddered at the horror the Lindberghs must be experiencing and the awful price they had paid for all that fame and hero-worship. It made me grateful for the advice Charles Lindbergh had given me and to soon be heading to the hallowed halls of Oxford University, the oldest English-speaking University in the world.

CHAPTER 25

Before I eventually left Victoria in 1934, both uncles had impressed upon me what an honour it was to attend Oxford.

"Oxford has been in existence for eight centuries, Caleb," began Uncle Bertie. "Just imagine all those who have walked its halls."

"And it has achieved eminence as a seat of learning and won the praises of popes and kings," added Uncle Teddy. "You are a fortunate young man, Cal. Since 1878, academic halls were also established for women, and they finally became members of the university in 1920." That fact alone made Oxford suddenly seem more interesting to me.

Granny Mac, however, had talked to me of other things concerning Oxfordshire itself and the surrounding area.

"I have never told you this before, Cal, but I was born in a village near Oxford called Great Noxley," she began one evening, as we sat in the drawing room after dinner. "I did not know who my parents were, and I was placed in an orphanage called Field House, which was adjacent to St. Mary's Church in the village. The home was run, in fact, by the Anglican Church. While you are over there, I would ask a favour of you."

"Of course, Gran, anything," I had said. I was astounded that she was confiding such a personal thing to me, because she had never before told me of her early life. I never realized she was an abandoned orphan.

"I would like you to find out if the Field House building is still in existence. I was there, of course, a long, long time ago, from 1845 until almost 1860, but I know the building was turned into a school afterward and may have long ago disappeared. I am sure, however, that St. Mary's Church would still be there, as would Noxley Manor, the country seat of the Sinclairs, where I first went into service. Seems so long ago ... and so silly to hide it now. It doesn't seem to matter anymore. Your grandfather found out the truth about my roots eventually." She paused for a long time. "Apparently I even came from the gentry. Imagine that ..."

"If I find Field House and the church, what would you like me to do, Gran?"

"I would like you to purchase a piano and donate it to them."

"A piano?"

"Yes, Cal, a piano. And also I want to set up an educational trust fund through the church for music. Could you do that for me?"

"As soon as I locate those places, I will let you know."

"Good, and then I will send the money and you can arrange it all through the legal channels. I think it would be nice to call it the Jane Hopkins Sheridan Musical Scholarship Fund, or something like that."

"Jane Hopkins Sheridan?"

"Yes, Jane Hopkins Sheridan. Now, don't ask any more questions, young man. Off you go and finish your packing. I'm missing you already."

I kissed her, thinking as I did so what an incredible lady she must have been and still was, and how little I really knew about her long-ago, mysterious past.

CHAPTER 26

For the next two years, I inhaled the atmosphere of Oxford University, a unique and historic institution.

I studied, as best I could. I made many friends and I had a great deal of fun, much of it involving adventurous escapades with members of the opposite sex. Although I was virtually still living the good life, I was also very aware of the economic times the world was experiencing, and especially what was happening in Europe. In those early years of the 1930s, none of us could have foreseen that another war with Germany was in our future, but the signs were all there, had we dared to look. Only in hindsight did we realize this.

During my first summer in Oxfordshire, I toured the beautiful Cotswold countryside with friends in a sporty Aston Martin, and we finally found the village of Great Noxley. Sure enough, St. Mary's Church dominated the village, and alongside it was the Fielding Elementary School. I enquired of an old-timer in the village, who was only too willing to relate the history of Great Noxley and the Sinclair family up at the Manor House.

"Oh, aye," he said. "Used to be an orphanage called Field House right over there where the Fielding Elementary School now stands. They closed down that home back in the 1870s, as well as the other workhouse at the opposite end of the village. It was closed down by the Sinclair family, it was. Them's the rich folk up at Noxley Manor. The family's still there, too. Made their money in textiles and the breweries, you know. Heard tell there was too much abuse going on at that little orphanage in the old days, though. Terrible it was."

"Who runs the school now?"

"St. Mary's," he replied. 'Tis run by the church, just like the orphanage was. You should go over and talk to the vicar, if you're interested."

"I will," I replied. "And thank you for your help."

The Reverend Moore at St. Mary's expanded on the history of Great Noxley and the orphanage that once occupied the site opposite the church. He was intrigued to know that my grandmother had been placed in that home so long ago, because apparently it had an infamous reputation in the village.

"It was a very good job that it was closed down. The church at that time was not aware of the atrocities that were taking place there, but of course those were different times. Thank goodness we have become more civilized today." He smiled.

I then told him my grandmother's wish concerning a music scholarship to be set up at the school and for a piano, the very finest, to be purchased for the students. He was overcome with joy and appreciation and insisted on me staying for tea at the vicarage. My two friends from university were also invited, and together we devoured the most enormous plate of dainty salmon and cucumber sandwiches, scones and little cakes prepared by the vicar's wife.

Afterwards I strolled around the church and the adjoining cemetery on my own. I wanted to take in the essence of the place where my grandmother had spent her childhood. She had mentioned a certain Reverend Lloyd, who was the Rector of St. Mary's when she was at Field House, so I scanned the list of names of past rectors inside the church. Sure enough, there was his name, *the Reverend Erasmus Lloyd, Rector of St. Mary's, 1840-1865.*

"Apparently he was the man who started my grandmother on the road to being a great pianist," I later told the present vicar.

"And now your dear grandmother has given back that gift she received as a child. It has come full circle," he replied. "We are so grateful and happy."

That night I wrote to Granny Mac with the news of my discovery and the arrangements that were being made to set up the scholarship fund and buy the piano. In her return letter to me, she simply said:

I have arranged for the transfer of funds to the church. Now at last, Cal, I am at peace with my past. Thank you, dearest, for indulging an old woman's wish. I'm going into the drawing room now and will play some Beethoven on the piano.

I felt good about what I had done.

* * *

In May of 1936, I returned to Canada, having completed a number of requisite courses at Oxford. I had had absolutely no interest or talent for the law, although I had become quite proficient in mathematics, music and English literature. But, needless to say, I shone best in aeronautical engineering.

It was a wonderful homecoming, and only when I wandered the acreage of Providence again did I fully realize how much I had missed my home. It always seemed to me that time stood still there and nothing really ever changed, although I knew in my heart that it did.

Granny Mac was now in her nineties, but she was still a healthy woman with a youthful attitude. Letty, at thirty-eight, was as attractive as ever, but also just as unapproachable as far as the male population went. Austin Harris seemed to have disappeared from the scene, and she had continued her nursing at the Royal Jubilee Hospital as well as taking care of Granny's needs at Providence and those of her own parents, Joe and Emily Caldwell, who still lived on St. Charles Avenue and were in reasonably good health.

Letty had continued to live at Providence even after I was grown up and no longer needed her maternal care. But it always seemed to me that Letty was destined to be a caregiver to everyone she met. Her sympathetic, warm, kindly soul had dictated her destiny in life.

The two uncles, in their sixties, were as dapper as ever. Uncle Teddy continued to dedicate his life to his many patients, who all adored him, and Uncle Bertie worked hard for the family business despite constantly threatening to retire.

"Been waiting for you to take over the reins, old chap," he told me on my first night home. I guess I was the Great White Hope for McBride's!

"Well, I'm more than ready and eager to take over the Airways division," I replied. "But I'm sure the rest of the company could run on its own with all the good management people you have."

And Letty's younger brothers, John and William, were both lawyers and now happily married. It seemed that practising law ran deep in the Caldwell blood. Hamilton House had been sold many years ago and the money put in a trust fund for me, part of which had paid my tuition at Oxford.

I was now ready to get back into flying for McBride's, but I was fully aware that things were changing by leaps and bounds in Canadian aviation. There was already talk of a trans-Canada airline for transporting passengers, and I envisioned McBride's being in the bidding war for such a contract. Meanwhile, our Airways Division continued to transport mail throughout Vancouver Island and the mainland.

Another type of flying, known as "bush flying," was becoming popular, and it was something that really excited me. The "bush pilot" had come into being in northern Manitoba, Ontario and Alberta, where you were literally in the "bush" the moment you took off. Flying into unmapped territory in British Columbia was something I had done frequently when barnstorming, but now I could see it as being a profitable way to open up British Columbia's northern interior.

"Why can't we transport surveyors and prospectors north, Uncle B?" I asked. "We could also take in medical supplies to remote areas. It must be feasible with these new Fairchild FC-2s and 71s that are being built. Many Fokker Universal, Wacos and Norseman are already in service, so I think we should buy some, too. They're designed specifically for the wilderness in North America. They're a very rugged aircraft, with enclosed, heated cockpits, more freight capacity, and other features to enable easier loading. Some have alternative undercarriages, wheels, skis or floats, so they can land in a variety of terrain and a variety of seasons. Why don't we give it a go?"

"All right, all right, I hear you, Cal," he said, laughing. "You've made your point, old chap. We'll look into it."

We did more than look into it. We purchased a fleet of the new bush planes, and within two months of my arrival home, McBride's Airways was in the bush pilot business in a big way, and I was heading the division.

* * *

The best part of bush piloting was being hired by prospectors who wanted to go into the interior to mine at an isolated lake or river. You then had to try your best to discover a reasonable place nearby to land, which was far from easy. There were no reliable maps, and a lot of it was pure guesswork. You also had to be sure you would be able to find your way out again, so it was an enormous challenge of both skill and cunning.

We also carried a great deal of freight into the north, and soon became familiar with the best and smoothest routes in and out of remote areas. Mostly the virgin terrain was rough, though, and unreliable at best. Small mountain ridges, uncharted lakes and the possibility of engine failure at any moment lent a certain amount of daredevil bravado to each operation we undertook.

Some people, especially those to whom we delivered much-needed medical supplies, considered us heroes. But in truth we were simply a bunch of fools doing a difficult job. The real heroes were the aircraft, which, time and again, proved their worth and saved our lives.

McBride's aircraft, along with their pilots, soon earned a reputation for being the best in the province, so we were constantly in demand even in the most northern regions, where we encountered the worst weather conditions, including the cursed ice factor.

Ice was our biggest enemy, and trying to de-ice propellers and wings was often a losing battle. There were various tricks involved, such as changing pitch and losing power, which would start the engines screaming and allow large chunks of ice to be thrown off the aircraft. That procedure sometimes solved the iced-up propellers, but the wings were a different matter altogether. Even the little inner tubes called "boots," which fitted over the nose of the each wing and were operated by an air pump, did not always solve the problem. The best solution was to simply try to escape cold temperatures as efficiently and quickly as possible before too much ice had formed. Unfortunately, however, ice forms so rapidly that before you know it, you have the equivalent weight of a two-by-four lying across your wing, all solid ice.

On one particular occasion, between Prince George and Fort St. John, my co-pilot and I were flying at about 11,000 feet. The air was clear and smooth and we were using instruments, all of which were working to perfection. Everything was running so effortlessly that I began to relax and eat my lunch.

Suddenly, a small crackling sound told us that a portion of ice had begun to form on one of the wings. But looking out, it appeared to be a mere sprinkle and nothing to worry about. I bent down in the cockpit to reach for another sandwich, and in that second, the plane felt like it had been hit by an enormous boulder.

"Hey, what the hell was that?" asked the co-pilot, who was somewhat of a novice.

"We've stalled and we're losing height," I replied. "Bloody right wing is completely covered in ice!" I tried to sound as calm as possible, but at the same time I realized the full potential of what we were up against, knowing that our speed was one hundred and forty-five miles per hour and the whole plane was quickly turning into a ball of ice.

Within the next thirty seconds, the plane lurched and dipped, and I yelled orders at the co-pilot to pile everything up against the left wall of the aircraft to even out our balance while I attempted to keep both engines running. But it was a losing battle.

With engines screaming at full pitch, we were dropping at an incredible rate, and I knew we were flying through mountains below the level of the peaks. Visibility was poor, and at any moment, we could hit one and it would all be over. When we somehow finally came out unscathed on the other side of the range and were nearing Fort St. John, the temperature was rising so rapidly that the ice all but disappeared. We managed to level out and return to normal. But for those few horrifying moments, our aircraft had turned into a distorted ball of ice with a will of its own, soaring through space. We had barely escaped with our lives.

Later we investigated the matter with the weather office back in Vancouver, but never did find the reason for such a sudden build-up of ice. We were two of the lucky ones that day. Others were not so fortunate, and many bush pilots lost their lives over the next few years in dense forest and uncharted mountainous terrain, often because their wings had iced up too quickly and made the aircraft uncontrollable.

It was a great life—if you didn't weaken.

CHAPTER 27

From 1936 until the end of 1938, McBride's Airways continued to be involved in the madness of bush flying. I made many forced landings myself, which some might consider crash landings. When your engine was failing, you had to be smart and quick to find a suitable field, open range or lake on which to land in a hurry. A couple of times I ended up in the trees, but the gods must have been on my side, because I always escaped with barely a scratch.

As North America began to slowly recover from the Depression, more people wanted to use flying as a means of travel, and it became obvious that a national Canadian airline would be needed. Canadian Airways, which was already providing regional passenger services in many areas, including the Vancouver to Seattle run, was in the market for establishing a national airline, as was the Canadian Pacific Railway, which had also been operating aircraft since 1919. I talked to Uncle Bertie about the possibility of McBride's Airways entering the bidding war, and he was enthusiastic about the idea.

Meanwhile, however, something else was developing in Europe that took up our attention and made us rethink all our priorities. We were beginning to suspect that another war was on the horizon.

"I forbid you to get involved, Cal," pleaded my grandmother as we all sat on the veranda one day that summer.

"I'm probably too old now anyway, Gran," I said. I was going to be twenty-eight that September and I knew that the first men to be called up were usually those between eighteen and twenty. "As a flyer, I'd be considered an old man."

"Good!" she said adamantly. "I will not have another of my grandsons involved in the madness of war."

"Well, Mother," interjected Uncle Teddy, "it will probably not come to that, anyway."

"Em! That's what everyone said in 1914, and look what happened then!" she retaliated. She was ninety-three years old that year and still as sharp as a tack and as feisty as ever. I admired her stamina, which was remarkable considering all she had been through in her long life.

In any event, the decision about becoming part of a transcontinental passenger airline, or joining the Canadian air force and getting involved in the likely war in Europe, was decided for us. Out of the blue, I received a call from a Flight Commander Jarvis with the RCAF. He wanted to meet with me in Vancouver to discuss the possibility of my heading a flight training school for young pilots in Alberta, Manitoba or Saskatchewan. The idea excited me, and I readily agreed to meet with him to discuss it.

Granny Mac was delighted with the idea. "Training pilots will be the answer," she said. "That way, you'll stay here in Canada and be out of the war in Europe if it comes." She patted my arm gently, and I smiled at her. But she knew me only too well not to ask me to make her any more definite promises beyond that.

Each time I left Providence and we said goodbye, I wondered if it would be the last time I would see her. The years were rushing by, and, although they had been kind to her physically, I knew that death comes to us all eventually. I felt an inner dread that one day Granny Mac would no longer be at Providence when I returned. It seemed inconceivable but, being realistic, I knew it was inevitable.

It was only after I left to meet Flight Commander Jarvis in September of 1938 that I realized she might well be having similar thoughts. Was she, too, wondering if it would be the last time we would be together? Would one of my crazy escapades end in my own death—even before hers?

I had made a promise to her and to myself that this time I would do my best to stay safe, and I meant it. I would not risk my life unnecessarily any more, causing her more pain. She had suffered enough in one lifetime, and I loved her far too much to cause her more.

Jarvis met me in Vancouver. He was a cordial, pleasant chap and spoke of my excellent reputation as a flight instructor in British Columbia from his knowledge of McBride's Airways.

"We've been trying to get people like you involved in this scheme since 1936, to enable us to get something going along these lines," he said. "Now at last the Brits want to get involved too, and an air training scheme has finally been put into place. Things are getting dicey in Europe, as you know, and they feel it might be a good idea to have these flight schools set up in Canada to train first-class pilots, in case we get pulled into this mess. We'll be a part of the British Commonwealth Air Training Plan, and we're setting up flight schools in most of the provinces. Are you interested, Hamilton?"

"It sounds like something in which I would most definitely be interested," I replied, without hesitation. "What planes are you using?"

"It depends on which school we post you to, but probably initially Harvards or the Canadian-built Avro 652A Ansons. There will be numerous flying schools across Canada, and we'd like you to head up one of them."

I was extremely flattered. It seemed that in one short moment, I had unofficially joined the RCAF and been promoted to Flight Instructor. Within a week, I was on my way to North Battleford, Saskatchewan, to begin training young men from all over the Commonwealth to become ace pilots.

For the next year, I devoted my time to training these young greenhorns the tricks of the trade, which basically meant teaching them everything I had been doing at our own flying schools at McBride's, plus some newer manoeuvres. We also did a lot of night flying and learning the textbook drills of dropping bombs on specific targets. These young pilots were men who would, if war should come, be risking life and limb to defend their country. They could not afford to make mistakes.

We formed a great camaraderie and I made many friends. When news came in September of 1939 that Germany had invaded Poland and Britain had declared war on Germany, we breathed a collective sigh of relief, because now we knew for sure that what we had been working on so diligently would finally be put to good use.

My work in Canada was far from finished, because new recruits were arriving daily. By May of 1940, when news came of the fall of France, I was beginning to realize that I would never be content to stay so far away from the action. In early September 1940, Germany began a strategic bombing campaign on London, targeting the most populated areas, the factories, and the dock yards.

I desperately wanted to be in Europe to help defend Britain. Having been brought up with an English/Scottish background, I felt a fervent blast of patriotism streaming through my blood. And also, in some deep-rooted place in my heart, I knew I needed to avenge my own brother's death so long ago.

But first I had to go back to Providence and face my grandmother. I was sure that this time she would understand.

CHAPTER 28

I will always remember the sight of her sitting there in her rocking chair on the veranda on that hot September afternoon in 1940, and to me she had never looked more beautiful. The sun was shining on her grey hair, tied back in her familiar bun, but I could still glimpse some speckles of gold among the grey. Her green eyes looked up at me as I walked toward her, and a smile lit up her face.

"Ah, Caleb," she said. "Come sit by me on the swing. I know you've come home to tell me something, haven't you?"

"Always so perceptive, you old devil," I responded.

"Hey, not so much of the 'old devil' now. Have some respect for your elders!"

"Well, Gran, I know you've told me you're going to be ninety-five this Christmas, but I simply don't believe you. You're still a kid at heart. So how can I possibly think of you as one of my 'elders'?"

"A *kid*? What kind of a word is that? Where do you come up with these expressions, Caleb?"

"Search me." I grinned as I sat down beside her and took her wrinkled little hand in mine.

"Now, are we just going to sit here and hold hands like a courting couple spooning under the moon, or are you going to tell me why you're really here?" she asked.

"I can't think of anything right now that I'd rather do than sit here and hold hands with you, Gran."

"Bah! Nonsense. You'd rather be out gallivanting with a stream of pretty young girls. 'Bout time you found yourself a real lady and settled down."

"You're absolutely right, old girl. But I doubt if anyone would ever have me."

"Then the girls you meet are simply not worth your time. You're just like your Uncle Bertie. He took up with all the wrong kind of women. Always did, and then it was too late. Don't leave it too late, Caleb."

"I won't, Gran. I promise."

"Promises, promises. You've made me a lot in your time, young man, and broken a few, too. Now, are you going to break another one, and go off to England to fight this damnable war? I see you're a Squadron Leader now, too. Pretty important stuff, eh?"

I was silent for a while. She had known my plans all the while. She was a crafty old bird.

Finally I nodded. "Yes, Gran, they want me in London. I'm to report to the Air Ministry later this month to form a bomber squadron."

She didn't reply for a while. "Is it set in stone?" she finally said.

"Well, I guess not. I could always turn it down."

"But you won't, will you?"

"No, Gran, I won't. It's something I have to do."

Neither of us spoke for a long time. We just sat there, holding hands and swinging back and forth in the late summer sunshine.

Finally she broke the silence. "Well, I suppose I will simply *have* to let you go. But this time, I insist you take this with you."

She began to pull on a thin leather strap from around her neck, which was tucked down beneath her dress. As she pulled it out from her clothing, I saw for the first time that, attached to the strap, was a rounded piece of metal.

"Your grandfather gave me this just before he died, Caleb. His mother in Scotland had given it to him when he left home for the first time as a young lad. It had belonged to his father, who always wore it round his neck for safety. Unfortunately, the night his father, your great-grandfather, was drowned off the coast of Scotland, he had left this talisman at home. Your great-grandmother always believed he would have survived that storm at sea had he had it with him that night."

"It has some words on it, Gran. What language is that?"

"It's Gaelic. In English it means, "Destiny will always bring you home." Your grandfather told me to wear it always because it would keep me safe, and he was absolutely right. But, you know, Caleb, I think I should have given it to Stephen when he left to fight in the Great War, or to your mother when she went north that time."

"You were not to know what would happen to them, Gran."

"Well, this time, I'm not taking any chances." Suddenly she bent the metal and snapped it in half. "See, you will take one half, and I'll keep the other half here."

"Oh Gran, you've spoiled it now."

"No, dear, I've merely separated the two halves until they can be joined again as one, and they will one day, because 'destiny' will bring them back together."

"Oh Gran, you're such a romantic old woman."

"Romantic? Well, I've never been accused of being romantic before. Too down-to-earth for that. Just realistic."

"Well, I think you're a romantic, Gran, and I will treasure this always and wear it around my neck as my lucky charm. I'll make a hole in this half and find another piece of leather or a chain for it. You keep yours, and I'll keep mine, and one day they will be back together again and made into one. That's a deal."

She squeezed my hand tightly. "Yes, dearest, that's a deal!"

Mrs. Potter came out then and brought us tea, and soon we were joined by Letty and the two uncles, as well as Dulcie, who was now in her late nineties. She had stayed on with us at Providence after her husband died and never returned to Salt Spring Island where some of her relatives still lived.

We laughed and joked together on that beautiful summer day, trying to erase from our minds the horrors of war taking place in Europe. Only once did Granny Mac refer to it by stating that she was sure that all the good men in the Allied forces would soon stamp out that evil man Adolf Hitler.

"Hear, hear," said the two uncles, and we all silently prayed her words would come true.

As she cleared away the tea things, Nell Potter could not refrain from adding her old familiar adage that we would all be in *dire straits* if Hitler was allowed to continue his rampage through Europe.

My grandmother, uncles, Letty and I were joined for dinner that night by Uncle James and Aunt Eliza Caldwell, William and his wife Liz, and John and his new wife, Sophie. Mrs. Potter served all of our favourite things. After dinner, we adjourned to the drawing room and Granny Mac played the piano for us for a while. Suddenly. she stopped and turned around on the piano stool to face me.

"Caleb, tonight I want you to play for us some of that modern popular stuff you enjoy. We need something cheerful to send you off on your way."

We were all surprised by her request, but I willingly got up and started to play a medley of all the popular songs of the day. I began with some Benny Goodman jazz and soon noticed that my grandmother's foot was beating time to the music. I mixed in a little classical stuff, too, but she soon put in more requests for the "modern" music, as she called it.

"Cal, I've heard you play "Begin the Beguine" sometimes, and what's that other one I like, about Paris?"

"April in Paris," I replied as I began another medley of her favourites. Then we all joined in singing "Nice Work if You Can Get It" and "I've Got My Love to Keep me Warm."

By then we were all in a merry mood and everyone was throwing in their requests. Then I had the urge to play a piece originally sung by Ella Fitzgerald back in 1936.

It was called "They Can't Take That Away from Me," and as I began it, I looked directly at my grandmother to the right and sang it especially for her. She was smiling at me and enjoying herself immensely.

All the words of the song, with its chorus of gratitude for the way she had changed my life, seemed to apply to this moment, and as she stood up slowly with the aid of her cane and came over to put her arms around me, she said, "Thank you, Caleb, that was wonderful. And now an old lady is going to retire to her bed. Good night, everyone."

We all got to our feet in deference to her, and with murmurs of "Goodnight, sleep tight," we watched her make her graceful exit from the room, like the queen that she was.

The next morning, after an early breakfast, I made my departure. None of us had ever been good at goodbyes, so our farewells were brief. Letty wished me well and said she would pray for my safety. My two uncles shook my hand a little too tightly and hugged me to them. Granny Mac had said everything she wanted to say the night before. As she took me in her arms, I noticed her half of the talisman was hanging outside her clothing and lay exposed on her breast. She clasped it firmly in one hand and pointed to my chest where, under my shirt, I was wearing the other half.

"Together again, one day," was all she said, and then she turned abruptly and went back into the house. Even the Potters looked sad, and I saw Nell Potter chase after my grandmother to comfort her, but she was waved off by Granny's hand.

I vowed to return to them all soon, and only after I had left and was well on my way did I realize that my grandmother had in fact never once said that *she and I* would be together again one day. Only that the two halves of our lucky talisman would somehow, in some way, miraculously be joined again as one in the future.

I had never felt quite so sad in my life. The last lines of the song I had sung especially for my grandmother, about how we might never meet again, though I would always remember, continued to ring in my ears long after I left Providence and started my journey.

PART THREE
(1941–1945)

The Arena of War
CAL, MAGGIE, JANE

CHAPTER 29

CAL

I returned to North Battleford in September of 1940, but my rendezvous in London and appointment at the Air Ministry was, for some unknown reason, delayed until early in 1941. I was growing extremely restless as I waited for orders to leave and could barely contain my impatience.

By then, London had been living for four months through the horrors of the blitz, which had begun on September 7, 1940. For fifty-seven consecutive nights, London was bombed relentlessly. Up until that point, the Luftwaffe had targeted only Royal Air Force airfields in an attempt to destroy the entire British air defence system. Now, their change of tactics and obvious disregard for civilians had incensed the British beyond belief. If it had been Hitler's plan to demoralize the British people with his strategic bombing campaign, it had had the opposite effect.

By the time I arrived in England in mid-January 1941, British morale was stronger than ever. The citizens of Britain were facing the enemy with resolute determination, and, despite the Nazi onslaught, Londoners and people of other targeted cities such as Portsmouth, Southampton, Bristol, Coventry, Nottingham, Norwich and Manchester, were carrying on with their lives as best they could, posting up "Business as Usual" notices outside their shops and homes. The British were more than ever determined not to allow the Germans to terrorize them into surrender.

Already the German air raids had killed more than 15,000 British civilians. Aside from London, one of the worst attacks had been in Coventry on the night of November 14, when four hundred and forty-nine German bombers had dropped 1,400 high-explosive bombs in addition to 100,000 incendiaries, flattening the city and killing more than five hundred, people with double that number injured.

The RAF, using the newly developed radar, had managed to inflict damage in return on the Luftwaffe bombers. RAF fighter planes had attacked incoming bombers with some success, as a result of which the Luftwaffe were never able to achieve air supremacy over England, which had been Hitler's prime objective before his proposed land invasion of England.

Despite this success by the RAF, there was still a great deal of work to do, and I was soon made very aware of this when I finally reported for duty at the Air Ministry in Whitehall on January 15, 1941.

The commander who met with me was not overly impressed by my credentials or the fact that I was a Canadian joining a Royal Air Force unit.

"I understand, Hamilton, that you wish to be involved in operations. Why?"

"I feel that I have exhausted my work on training units and would now like to offer my services in bombing operations, sir," I replied.

"Well, Hamilton, you realize that you will immediately be demoted to Flight Lieutenant. None of this Squadron Leader stuff anymore. You have to earn that rank back in ops."

"Yes, sir, I understand that."

"And to begin with, I am posting you to an Operational Training Unit, where it will be your duty to take part in a twenty-hour flying course with nine other men. You will all be trained in daytime and night-time flying, and of course flying in formation."

What the hell did this idiot think I'd been doing for the past two years at North Battleford, and for years before that as a bush pilot?

I wanted to be in ops so badly, however, that I did not argue. If it meant eating humble pie for a while, so be it.

* * *

I was posted to an air base in Norwich and joined Unit Number 13. There were seven Canadians, one chap from New Zealand, and two Brits in the unit. No one complained about our unit number. You couldn't afford to be superstitious in wartime.

On my first night at the base, I realized we were one Canadian short, so I enquired of the others if anyone knew when he would be arriving. No one did.

The next morning, we all assembled in the crew room for a pep talk from one of the commanding officers. As we awaited his arrival, the door suddenly burst open and a rather dishevelled, obviously hung-over chap entered. He looked around and then made eye contact with me, and we both started to laugh. God help me, if it wasn't my old pal Charlie Fuller!

"Mac!" he screeched. "What the hell are you doing here?"

"Charlie, you asshole! You look like hell. Are you part of this unit? Are *you* the missing Canadian?"

"Well, if this is Number 13, and we're in Norwich, England, I guess this is where I'm supposed to be!"

We shook hands, hugged and thumped each other on the back. Everyone was looking at us, obviously thinking what a crazy pair of Canucks we were, when the door opened again and Commanding Officer Riddleton entered. We all stood to attention to await his pep talk.

Something about him got my back up from the start. He was supremely standoffish, and many of his remarks were just plain offensive. He delighted in putting us all down with remarks like, "Where the bloody hell were you blokes when we needed you last year?" and "I suppose as you are all part of this great Commonwealth Training Program, you think you're something special and know it all."

I took as much as I could. Apart from Charlie and I, who at age thirty-one were already old men as far as wartime recruits went, most of the men in the unit were young fellows between the ages of nineteen and twenty-two, and they deserved better than this. Someone had to say something on their behalf.

When he paused briefly in his so-called pep talk, I stood up and addressed him. "May I say something, Commander Riddleton?" I asked respectfully.

"Name, rank and number!" he bellowed back.

"Squadron ... I mean Flight Lieutenant Hamilton, #85657, sir."

"Speak up, Hamilton!"

"I was under the impression that your lecture this morning was supposed to be a pep talk, sir, to boost our morale, so to speak, but much to my surprise I am finding it a most demoralizing diatribe of utter nonsense!"

There were a few gasps and some throat-clearing around the room. Some of the men adjusted position, scraping their chairs on the concrete floor as they did so.

"I beg your pardon! I hope I didn't hear you right, but if I did, just what is your problem, *Flight Lieutenant Hamilton?*" He emphasized my rank, obviously aware that I had been demoted upon arrival in England.

"I have no problem, sir, but I think you should know that these young men have all been very anxious to risk their lives for their country for a very long time now. And, as to where we were when you needed us, most of us were bloody well training our asses off to be the best damned pilots we could be. A little appreciation on your part that we are finally here might have been nice."

"Appreciation? You want appreciation? Well, Hamilton, I've news for you. This is war and it's no bloody picnic, so you men had better do a damn good job over the next few months, and then, and only then, will you see any appreciation from me. You have to prove yourself here in training before you'll even be going on any sorties against the enemy, Hamilton, so you can forget about what a bloody star you once were back in Canada. Is that clear?"

"Perfectly clear, sir!" I replied. "And I doubt if you will be disappointed in our skills. We're all good, damn good!"

His lip curled up at one side. I couldn't decide if it was a sneer or a smile. "I don't need words, Hamilton. I need proof."

With that, he retrieved the papers he had placed on the desk, put his baton under his arm and marched briskly out of the room.

As the door slammed behind him, everyone cheered and thumped me on the back.

"Well said, Mac! He needed taking down a peg or two."

"Well, you really told *him* his fortune, mate," added one of the Brits.

Suddenly I had become the hero in the group and, unwittingly, they had made me their designated leader. From that day on, I felt an almost fatherly responsibility for them all.

In return, it wasn't long before they proved time and time again that they were willing to follow me into hell and back—little knowing that that was exactly what they would be doing.

CHAPTER 30

For the next six weeks, we followed the textbook training course to the letter. We flew in daytime, we flew at night, we flew in fog and rain, and in other worse wintery conditions, and we did formation flying.

We also learned everything about one another, because we spent twenty-four hours a day together. We slept in the same quarters, ate together, drank together and argued together. We also laughed a lot. You had to keep a sense of humour if you intended to survive.

Before long, we all had nicknames. I was known as "Skipper" or "Crazy Mac" from my barnstorming days, and Charlie became "Sir Charles" because of his somewhat overdeveloped English/Torontonian accent. The other five Canadians were Pete Pegrum (known as "Peg"); Daniel Hoy ("Danny Boy"); Ben Masters ("The Stud"—for reasons that soon became obvious); Jimmy Marshall ("Jock") and our youngest member, eighteen-year-old Billy Benson ("Junior"). Our chap from New Zealand was Eric Porter, who was never without his pipe and its rather foul smelling tobacco. We nicknamed him "Baccy". The two British chaps were Barney White ("Chalky") and Edward Thomas Green ("Tommy").

Finally, our motley crew was considered ready for operations. We didn't always fly together, because there were only six or seven in a flight crew: the pilot, navigator, flight engineer, bomb aimer, wireless operator, and one or two gunners (mid-upper and rear gunner, fondly referred to as ass-end Charlie). Sir Charles, Stud and I were the pilots, Peg was a navigator, Danny Boy, Jock and Junior were gunners, Baccy was the bomb aimer, and Chalky and Tommy were both flight engineers and wireless operators.

On my first test, a night flight over France dropping supplies of arms, ammunition, food and medical necessities to the underground movement at very specific targets, I had Peg as my navigator and Chalky as flight engineer. We took along Baccy as the bomb aimer and Junior as ass-end Charlie, even though we were not specifically planning to bomb any targets on that operation. We passed that first test with flying colours.

Other operations involved flying in formation in boxes of six. I was usually number four, with Sir Charles flying number two and Stud number five. Soon we were involved in testing our skills, flying at low levels underneath the flak from the Hun, an interesting and sometimes frustrating exercise.

One particular operation I vividly recall was a bombing attack on a Panzer Division headquarters in France. We had received word that thirteen German generals were holding a top-level meeting at a specific French chateau, which was to be our target that night. We successfully managed to hit the target spot on and eliminate all thirteen generals.

Despite the inevitable horrors of war, we all felt redeemed that night. We were finally making a difference.

CHAPTER 31

JANE (Victoria)

I wrote to Cal every week. Sometimes they were just short missives because my arthritic hands were playing up.

Only playing the piano seems to loosen up my hands, I wrote. *I would love to hear you play again, Caleb—even some of that new modern stuff.* I smiled as I wrote that, remembering our last night at Providence together.

Letty wrote longer letters every month, and she kept Cal up to date with everything going on at Providence. Sometimes I wondered if she told him anything about Austin Harris. I think they had parted company, but I didn't know for sure because she never spoke of him to me.

The twins also added a page or two in with my letters occasionally, and I enjoyed reading their wry comments about the stupidities of war. They nonetheless managed to retain their patriotism.

Wish we could be there with you fighting the good fight, old boy, they frequently wrote, and again I thought how very reckless men were. Could they not see how senseless war was? People killing one another for no apparent reason.

But Letty sat with me often, and she helped me to understand why men were that way.

"Granny Mac, don't you see that we have to fight for what is right in the world? We did it in the Great War and now we must do it again because of the evil spreading throughout Europe."

"Ah yes, that wicked man Adolf Hitler. I suppose you are right, Letty. He cannot be allowed to do what he is doing."

"And we can do something back here, too. I've been working with the Red Cross, rolling bandages and packing up parcels of goodies for people in Britain."

"Oh, what a wonderful idea, Letty. Can I help? I remember years ago, when I first started doing charity work with the help of the church to assist poor, single women with a child to support. It was so rewarding."

"Do tell me about it, Granny Mac. I'd be so interested. I've brought some bandages to roll, so perhaps we could work on that while you tell me."

I knew what she was doing—trying to take my mind off what was happening in Europe and whether Cal was safe or not.

I enjoyed telling her about the ladies who had donated money and clothes back then. I even shared a little of my history. Other than with Gideon and Dulcie, I had rarely talked about my past. After a while, I felt confident in asking her a question.

"What happened to that nice young man who used to visit you, Letty? Wasn't his name Austin?"

"Yes. He went back to his home in Calgary."

"What a shame."

"A shame?"

"Well, I thought he might propose to you eventually."

"He did."

"And?"

"Granny Mac, I cared about him a lot but ..."

"You still loved Stephen?"

"Yes. So I let Austin down gently. He deserved someone who could love him completely—the way I loved Steve."

"I understand, my pet. But oh, what a shame! You might well have grown to love him in time. You could have had a family of your own with him. Stephen would have wanted you to be happy."

"I am happy, Granny Mac. Nursing. Helping you raise Cal, taking care of you and my parents. It was meant to be that way."

"Hmmh ... always the nurse. But maybe there could still be time?

She looked at me strangely. "Time for what?"

"Oh I don't know. Destiny to work its magic?"

She smiled. "It already did, dear Granny Mac. It was meant for me to stay here in Victoria with you all. I don't need another family to make me happy."

CHAPTER 32

CAL

I wrote letters back to my family when I could, but needless to say I left out a lot of the more graphic details in the letters I sent to Granny Mac.

I did tell Letty everything, mainly to unburden myself, but I knew that she would understand what I was going through, having witnessed war and all its horrors herself many years earlier. We were there for a specific purpose, but that did not make killing the enemy any easier.

As we completed more operations, bombing specific targets such as bridges, railway lines and trains carrying German troops, we often took along two gunners on each trip as an extra precaution. We flew many night raids, because daytime ops often meant terrible losses from the flak of anti-aircraft fire and from German fighter planes. Trouble was, night-time flying had the additional problem of not being able to accurately locate our target.

Nonetheless, throughout 1941 and well into 1942 we continued to pursue the Hun and, at the same time, help keep the British morale high. Meetings back in the crew room showed, however, that our attempts were far from being a rousing success. Only one in every five aircraft was dropping its bombs within eight kilometres of the target. Not a good record. It was then decided that Bomber Command should aim for larger targets, such as Germany's big cities, and Churchill's advisers thought that dropping bombs on civilians would break the German spirit, just as Hitler had thought his blitzkrieg of 1940 would break the British. Thus we began a strategic bombing offensive against Germany.

Within a few months, I had completed my first "tour" of thirty bombing operations, after which I had the choice of serving another tour or becoming an instructor at an Operational Training Unit. I opted for another tour in Bomber Command and won back my rank of Squadron Leader.

It was Commander Riddleton himself who gave me the news.

"You've proved your words with action, Hamilton," he said. "Well done!"

"Thank you, sir," I replied, and I could not resist adding, "I told you we were all damn good."

This time he did smile. "Yes, you most certainly did, in no uncertain terms! I stand corrected."

From then on, there was a sort of guarded respect between us. When my citation came through from the Air Ministry, I sent it home to my grandmother, because I knew she would enjoy seeing it. It read as follows:

This officer has proved that he possesses a standard of efficiency and sense of duty of the highest order, which have been a constant example to all those with whom he comes in contact. He has shown outstanding ability as an instructor, Flight Commander and Examining Officer, and can be relied upon to carry out any task allotted to him in a very thorough manner.

Late in 1943, I was able to send home even better news. An Air Ministry bulletin arrived at the mess one day, telling me I had been awarded the Distinguished Flying Cross with a citation attached that read:

Squadron Leader Hamilton has completed numerous sorties against the enemy. His keenness and determination on all occasions have set a fine example to the other members of his Squadron. On one occasion before reaching his target he was subjected to heavy and accurate anti-aircraft fire and one engine failed. Despite this, he pressed on and successfully completed his mission. Throughout, Squadron Leader Hamilton has proved himself to be a most successful flight commander and by his untiring efforts and skill he has contributed much to the success achieved by his squadron.

In my letter to Granny Mac, I added:

Of course these chaps exaggerate a great deal! It was just a routine sortie, nothing special and I made it back home easily. The lucky talisman helped though—I wear it always—and I know it keeps me safe."

I refrained from adding that the particular "occasion" referred to in the citation was anything but ordinary and only a bloody fool would have attempted what I did on that miserable, wet day in August of 1943. The reality was far from normal and I had literally survived it on nothing but a wing and prayer, plus a little help from my half of the talisman still hanging around my neck.

* * *

This is what actually happened.

The night before, we'd held an inebriated bash in the officers' mess and were all very hung-over when we returned to our beds and crashed for what we hoped would be a long night of oblivion.

Minutes later, it seemed, although in actuality it was about three hours, a hammering on the barracks door began and would not quit.

"Stop that goddamn racket!" screamed Peg. "There are guys here trying to sleep!"

The hammering continued.

As their leader, I knew I had to rouse myself sufficiently to find out what was going on. It could be important, so, groping around in the dark at an unsteady pitch, I opened the door to see a dripping wet dispatch rider grinning from ear to ear, obviously enjoying his job of having to wake up a dozen or more hung-over men.

"Your presence is required immediately, sir, in the ops room. Urgent! You're to bring your best navigator, a wireless operator, a bomb aimer and two gunners as crew. Top secret mission, sir." *God, weren't they all?*

I started yelling at everyone, forcing them to head through the drizzle to the ablutions room, a primitively constructed building open to the elements, where we knew from experience that turning on taps for hot water was useless. If we'd had the next thousand years to spare, I doubt if cold water would ever have turned to even lukewarm. That night my crew would be Peg, Danny Boy, Junior, Baccy and Chalky, and at least the cold water woke us all up in a hurry. Sir Charles and the Stud were busy forming their own crews.

I was already wishing I had refused that last pint the night before. My watch showed 0350 hours by then. A quick breakfast and an even quicker briefing, and we were heading to the airfield and about to take off in formations of six Mitchells, the second of which I was leading with my crew. By all accounts, this night was going to be a maximum effort and involved a number of squadrons. We would all meet on the south coast to concert our efforts and facilitate an umbrella cover for the fighter boys.

Our target was to be an ammunition dump south of Rouen. It was an important target vital to the retreating army, but we knew it would be ringed with anti-aircraft guns. With our usual bravado, we gave each squadron the thumbs-up sign, telling each other it was going to be a piece of cake.

We managed to dodge most of the flak crossing the French coast, which was now almost routine, and we easily made it to 17,000 feet. I checked our position with Peg and Chalky, and things seemed to be going well. Baccy lay in his usual prone position in the tunnel beneath my seat, ready to release the bombs from the bomb bay, and Danny Boy and Junior were at the ready in their gunnery positions.

Suddenly I noticed that for some reason the port motor oil pressure was dropping and the cylinder head temperature had literally risen off the clock. I heard Sir Charles's voice coming from number two position in the formation, directly below me.

"Hey, Mac, there's oil and sundry other muck leaking from your kite, and it's covering my Perspex. Forward vision obliterated. What's up?"

"Thanks, Charlie. Looking into the problem," I replied.

Number 5, piloted by the Stud, was positioned on my starboard wing tip, so I signalled for him to take the lead, which allowed me to pull up and away, out of the formation. I was still somehow managing to hold height and keeping on course.

Pretty soon, however, the port motor was vibrating like crazy and all my instruments told a sorry story. Rather than risk a seize-up, which would have prevented the feathering of the propeller or, even worse, created a fire, forcing us to abandon the aircraft over enemy territory, I decided to shut down that motor completely, thereby losing considerable altitude. Despite a full bomb load, the old girl continued to waffle along quite well.

Our problems by then were only too obvious to the enemy. We were now the lame duck in the pack, so they became hell-bent on concentrating an all-out attack on us. Danny Boy and Junior were put to the test as I did my best to weave and duck, but one glance at the starboard motor readings told me I was flogging the Mitchell far too hard, so I eased back on the throttle to stop her overheating.

It was now clear that we could not maintain height without fear of stalling, and I had to make some pretty quick decisions. Should I proceed, as gently as possible at a safe speed and put up with some gradual height loss, enabling the enemy to bombard us even more, or should I dump the bombs now?

According to Peg, we were still on a track that was taking us right across the forward Allied lines, so to jettison the bombs there and then would risk carnage on either the British or the Canadians on the ground and wipe out some French villages in the process.

I yelled at Peg: "How many minutes to our target?"

"Twelve," he yelled back, "but you must be bloody mad to continue on to target on only one engine."

I ignored him. "Baccy, get ready, and when we reach the target, for Christ's sake make sure you dropped all spot on!!"

There was silence for a moment while everyone took this in. I tried to make light of it. "Well, guys, I always was crazy! Let's just hope it pays off this time."

According to Junior, the other formations were returning by then, having dropped their bombs. They were swanning off home in good order. It suddenly felt very lonely in the cockpit. I grasped my talisman.

"Well, old girl, we'll see if this thing really works now, won't we?" I whispered.

There were no longer any fighter boys around to give us cover, either. They were heading home too, probably assuming we had crashed by now and there was nothing more they could do. We had been in a similar position on numerous occasions in the past, watching our colleagues dive to their deaths or bail out and be captured in enemy territory.

The shell bursts around us increased. Obviously the Hun was venting its spleen on the lame duck again. Trying to dive out of the way of the flak lost us more valuable height.

Junior, a French Canadian and a staunch Catholic, began to say his rosary. I told him it was getting on my nerves.

"Stop counting your bloody beads and start firing, Junior." He obeyed me automatically without question.

Finally, after what seemed like hours but was really only minutes, Peg's voice announced: "Over target … now, sir."

"Bombs away, Baccy!" I yelled, and he let go the bomb load, dead on target. We could not possibly have missed it, because by that time we were down to five thousand feet.

I then quickly veered to the right in hopes of swinging the aircraft over the Canadian line and thereby gaining some protection, but enemy fire kept pounding us, and now machine gun fire had joined the fray. The poor old girl was handling a little better now without her bomb load, but all the violent evasive action I had put her through had demanded full power, which, in turn, had overheated the starboard motor. We were still losing altitude. Each time I tried to recover a foot or two, she rapidly reached the point of stall.

With adrenalin running high and my bowels long since having turned to water, I somehow managed to turn her around on course for home while running the gauntlet of enemy fire. It seemed like a lifetime before the Hun finally quit firing at us, and by then we were down to less than one thousand feet again. That was when I spotted the French coast coming up straight ahead. My gunners had fired off most of their ammunition to lighten our load even more, and I was finally beginning to feel a little less panicky.

Our troubles, however, were far from over.

CHAPTER 33

Peg gave me a course correction that would bring us out over the Channel and just slightly to the right of the well-established beachhead. I immediately began to tinker with my instruments, trying to think of all possible ways to cool down the overheated motor, while at the same time calculating our chances of getting across the Channel on very low fuel. A wide-open throttle for so long had more than doubled fuel consumption. I was so engrossed in this problem that I wasn't paying much attention to the terrain below us.

Suddenly I realized we were exiting France directly over Le Havre. I remembered too late that our quick pre-op briefing had included the information that the Germans were still tenaciously holding that town, despite being surrounded by our forces. Needless to say, the garrison enemy, having spotted us, were now venting a little more spite our way.

Miraculously we managed to fly through that dilemma, only to spot a small flak ship bristling with guns, all ready to also fire on us. We dodged about in that fracas until we were down to a mere five hundred feet and heading out to sea. There was great doubt in my mind by now as to whether we would make it to an airfield on the south coast of England. If I decided to shift fuel from the port tanks, where there was still plenty, over to the starboard motor by using the fuel transfer valve, that action alone could create an airlock in the system and thereby choke the flow of fuel to the good motor.

By then, I figured we would have to ditch, but with a clear sight of the very rough seas below, I decided I owed my crew a better chance of survival than that. I must admit that my own skin was also pretty important to me, so, without more ado, I decided to turn left and head for the emergency landing strip located just inland from the beachhead. At least that is where we had been told it was at our briefing.

We spotted the landing strip and headed straight for it. By then my eyes were burning and my arms and legs, with all the twisting and turning I had done, felt like hell. Forgetting the balloon barrage and the swinging cables, I went directly over the beachhead and manoeuvred the old girl towards the landing strip. The strip had been constructed of plates of steel laid over undulating ploughed fields. I knew it would be like landing on a roller coaster. In that final moment, I prayed there would be no malfunction to my wheels, because if they didn't release, the belly of the Mitchell would be torn out and the ensuing fire would mean it was all over for us.

We were lucky. The wheels released, and we made a real pansy-one motor landing. My crew yelped with delight and we all let out a collective sigh of relief. We immediately exited the aircraft like a bunch of excited schoolboys, laughing and slapping one another on the back. Them I sat for a moment watching my crew, hearing them calling to me but wanting this short moment to myself. I was feeling more than a little emotional.

I squeezed the talisman in my right hand. "Thanks, old girl," I said to my grandmother, thousands of miles away.

The group captain of the fighter wing operation on the strip came out to greet us, explaining that they were under extreme pressure at the moment. *Who isn't,* I wondered.

"We can only loan you guys a jeep and some food but little else at the moment, I'm afraid," he said. They didn't even have a working radio link with the U.K. to report our whereabouts.

I inspected the Mitchell thoroughly and saw that she had sustained a great deal of damage, and there was little hope I would be able to fly her back to home base. It was also clear where our troubles had originated. The main oil feed was cleanly severed, which must have been caused by the flak we took when we initially crossed the French coast.

With no ground crew available and no spare parts, we were obviously going to be stranded there for a while. Royal Air Force regulations stated that aircrew were not allowed to fiddle with an aircraft themselves. That was the sole domain of ground crew, so I could not even borrow a spanner to put my kite right.

While we were sitting around debating our troubles, a plane came in to land. I recognized it immediately from my North Battleford days as being an old Anson. What I could not have imagined in a thousand years was seeing the pilot who emerged from the cockpit: none other than Commander Jarvis, the man who had first enrolled me in all this madness back in 1938.

The "old pals" act worked wonders. Neither of us could believe the irony of our meeting in such a place in such a situation, he being there to check on some of the fighter planes, and me being there through pure luck by guesswork and by God.

"I'd be happy to fly you and your crew back to Blakehill, Mac," he said. "From there I can arrange for another pilot to fly you back to your base."

Tired, dirty, our throats raw from shouting over the noise of shelling and flak, we could have kissed his feet in gratitude. Our relief and thanks were overwhelming.

But an amusing incident at Blakehill provided a great deal of fodder for jokes in the mess later that night. As we landed there, we were confronted by a character covered in gold braid who informed us he was a customs officer.

He looked us all over very suspiciously and then asked, "Have you anything to declare?"

Dirty, smelly and on the point of exhaustion, I choked back my irritation, trying at the same time not to explode with indignation.

"Good God, man, I suppose if this had been an invasion, you'd have asked the bloody Germans the same question!"

His face coloured, suddenly realizing his stupid mistake for not having fully understood what we had just gone through over the past twenty-four hours.

By the time we arrived back at the mess, the bar had long-since closed, but it was very promptly reopened for drinks all round. We had been assumed "missing in action," and personnel were already preparing the necessary telegrams to be sent to our next-of-kin.

Charlie, who was more than a little emotional at seeing my ugly mug again, summed it all up brilliantly.

"Who else but a completely crazy moron like you, Mac, would have attempted to continue on a bombing mission with only one motor operating?"

I must admit I began to wonder the same thing myself.

In any event, the result of that particular escapade was why I was being awarded the Distinguished Flying Cross, but in truth I felt that it really belonged to every one of us.

CHAPTER 34

One month later, I was posted up North on radar exercises. Little radar boxes were attached to our aircraft equipped with wires that showed us the exact location at which we were aiming, enabling more precise bombing of a specific target.

By November, I was back again at home base and putting these wonderful contraptions into full use. Throughout the winter of 1943-44, we continued our bombing raids. Many were enormously successful, while others were abysmal failures, but certainly Mr. Radar now helped our cause.

Reading through my log entries after an operation always made me smile. As pilots, we tended to make light of the most atrocious circumstances in which we found ourselves, and we abbreviated enormous disasters to a stupid degree. I laughed at some of the comments I had written, such as "fuel dump uneventful," "swamped in fog," or "bombs stuck in the bay," as well as "touchdown dicey on wet grass" and "abandoned aircraft on landing."

The truth of those log entries was a completely different story, and had I had the time or inclination to write all the details, I might have added that the fuel dump had to be timed to the second and set everyone's nerves on edge, and that we were flying for what seemed like hours through an unknown hell in that pea-souper of a fog, and when the bombs got "stuck" in the bomb bay, Baccy improvised with a long broomstick to try to dislodge the damn things, knowing that at any second we might all be blown to hell and back.

My touchdown on wet grass was also somewhat more hair-raising than it sounded. The aircraft skidded wildly right off the runway, causing the belly of our trusted kite to land in the mud. We missed a large concrete construction by inches and took off part of our right wing in the process. Abandoning aircraft involved running like clappers from hell, despite terrible fatigue. Then, at a safe distance from the craft, I counted my crew to find I was one short. Panic ensued until Junior appeared through the darkness, hobbling on one leg but grinning from ear to ear.

My squadron now led many of the formations on operations, and I was also given new crews from time to time. Some of these men were good, some mediocre and some just plain idiots. I preferred my own men. As pilots, we were given instructions in code involving location sites, and the codes were written on rice paper. We were told that if we were captured, we should eat the paper.

I also spent a lot of time in the Operations Room, my job then being to worry about my men and sometimes to guide them back to safety. I hated losing men, but all too often I witnessed the malfunctioning of an engine having been hit by anti-aircraft fire, and then silence, knowing that one of our men and his crew were in the drink.

Commander Riddleton went on one particular op and got a terrific beating. One of his engines faltered, causing some distress and a certain amount of panic. I was in the control room that night and heard him calling for assistance. His starboard motor was backfiring, and part of his engine had fallen away. The undercarriage had completely gone and he was coming in for a belly landing. We guided him down, but he skidded for approximately three-quarters of a mile before coming to a stop. Trucks, jeeps and ambulances rushed to his assistance, to get him and his crew safely out. His face appeared slowly from the cockpit, and he was laughing his head off. Never mind that his aircraft was a write-off. He had brought his crew safely home, and that was all that counted for him. He established himself that night with the entire squadron as a damned good fellow.

In January of 1944, the Luftwaffe once again began a series of heavy attacks on British targets, including London. Some of our Mosquito night-fighters, equipped with radar, accounted for at least a hundred and twenty-nine of the three hundred and twenty-nine German aircraft shot down during that five-month attack, and by February the Allies were beginning a bombing campaign second to none in retaliation. We in turn were aiming for the French railway system, in an attempt to disrupt the Germans' reinforcement plans. We all knew we were heading into the forthcoming invasion plan of Europe.

In March, our Lancasters and Halifaxes in Bomber Command began another offensive against the German transport network in occupied Europe, and we continued to target the railway yards in France. Bomber Command was allocated thirty-seven of the eighty specific targets. We had many successes, but by the end of the month we had also experienced great losses, some of them very personal to me. The Stud was shot down over France and reported killed in action. And on the night of March 30, in a massive attack on Nuremberg, Bomber Command suffered its heaviest loss of the war so far. Ninety-five aircraft failed to return after being attacked by German night-fighters.

Charlie and I were two of the lucky ones who came back, but suddenly we both felt sickened, depressed and exhausted, and we began to question what the hell it was all about, and whether the pain and horror of so much carnage was really worth it in the greater scheme of things.

We were both due for leave, and this time we didn't hesitate to take it. We needed a break and were determined to head for London and spend the next five days drinking, womanizing and living life to the full, as though there was no tomorrow—for who knew, there most probably would not be.

CHAPTER 35

Our leave began once we caught the Norwich train for London at four o'clock in the afternoon of April 1, 1944. We would have preferred to rent a car and drive through the countryside of Norfolk, Suffolk and Essex on our way to London, but with the petrol shortage and limited restrictions everywhere, this proved impossible.

The train stopped in Colchester and was then supposed to head straight through to London. Soon after leaving Chelmsford in Essex, the train began slowing and making frequent short stops. When it reached a place called Grange Park, it screeched to a complete halt and all the lights on the train went out.

We sat in relative darkness for a few minutes because the evening light was by then drawing in. Suddenly, an air raid warden yelled at all the passengers from the platform.

"Disembark here, please. Air raid. Air raid. Head for the nearest shelter. This way ..."

None of us had heard a siren, but we didn't question the warden. I guess he knew best. Charlie and I jumped off the train and ran with everyone else toward the shelter.

"What a piece of irony if we cop it right here on the ground, Mac," Charlie said, laughing.

"After all we've been through, pal, those bloody Hun are not gonna get us this way," I replied.

We all waited in the shelter for over an hour but heard no sound of bombing or shelling. We came to the conclusion it had all been a false alarm, and eventually the all-clear siren sounded and we were told to leave the shelter.

"Hey, Charlie, it's a bit late to continue on to London now. We'd never find accommodation at this hour. Why don't we stay here? There must be a pub nearby with rooms to rent."

"Sounds good to me, pal."

"Try The Fox & Hounds, fellows," suggested a guy standing nearby. "I know the people who run it. Nice folk. I'm sure they'd put you up for the night."

He gave us directions and we began to walk away from the station and up the hill to the pub. It was now past seven o'clock, so we hoped they would have a room that night. I wasn't feeling particularly cheerful when we arrived at the pub and pushed open the door, but at least it was warm inside. A fire was blazing in the fireplace, despite this being so-called spring and coal being scarce or non-existent. Someone was playing "The White Cliffs of Dover" on the piano and singing very off-key, as we headed over to the bar and addressed the landlord.

"Any chance of getting a room for tonight?" I asked.

"Think we could manage that, mate," the landlord replied.

"Anything for you boys in blue," added a rather blousey-looking blonde I presumed was his wife. She smiled at us. "Now, you boys look like you could do with a good strong drink?"

I winked at her. "A pint of your best, honey," I replied.

She studied our uniforms. "RAF boys and yet an American accent? How come?"

Charlie rose to the occasion with dignity. "*Canadian* accent, sweetheart!"

"Ooops, sorree! We get so many Yanks in here from the nearby base. I just assumed ... you do sound all the same, you know."

Charlie and I raised our eyebrows. "Well, we'll just have to teach you how the Canucks really talk, honey!"

She produced two large pints of beer and suggested a table in the far corner. "Less crowded over there, ducks. My hubby will make sure there's a nice room ready for you whenever you want it, and he'll take up your bags. Enjoy your drinks."

We headed for the so-called quiet corner, but it was still pretty noisy. The piano player was grating on my nerves by now. He was hitting too many bad keys. The bar was reasonably pleasant, though, with its traditional low oak beams and old world ambience, and it was certainly warm. At least we were getting a break from the all the horror and tension of the past few weeks.

I looked down into my beer, and neither Charlie nor I spoke for a while. It seemed too much effort to shout above the cacophony all around us. For some reason I fished out my talisman from around my neck and gripped it tightly in my right hand as I thought of Providence and everyone back home.

I was suddenly so sick of war. I was sick of all the flying, the bombing, the killing in operation after operation, the total destruction, and the never-ending Hun slaughtering us. I was sick of the whole damn war without an end in sight.

I hated it all, and being on leave in this godforsaken place on the night of April 1—the irony of that date only came to me later—even with my good pal Charlie did not seem to alleviate my depression. I wanted desperately for it all to be over. And I wanted to go home.

Then something made me look up across the crowded room, and for a moment time stood still. Everything was suddenly happening in slow motion because I had made eye contact with the most enchanting woman I had ever seen. She raised her head at precisely that same moment and was looking at me. She seemed to colour slightly, perhaps in embarrassment, as our eyes made contact.

Her hair was a fascinating shade of auburn, cut unfashionably short with a delightful wave in the front that fell across her forehead and which she now flicked backwards. Her bobbed hair was shiny and made me want to run my fingers through it. Most women at that time wore their hair in what I considered an ugly style, swept back on each side with the aid of combs. But this woman was different. She was incredibly beautiful in a simple, unadorned fashion, and I knew immediately that I wanted to get to know her.

Because suddenly I realized, beyond a shadow of a doubt, that even though geographically I was thousands of miles away from Providence, I had finally come home.

CHAPTER 36

MAGGIE

I noticed him the moment he came in, and it was most embarrassing, the way he kept staring at me.

He was signalling the barmaid, and I heard her ask him, "Another round, luv?" He appeared to be asking her something. They both looked over at me, and the other man with him was shaking his head and smiling.

The barmaid, Flossie, had a loud voice, so I heard her say to him, "Oh the pretty lass? That's Maggie Graham. The other gal in uniform is her sister, Beth Winters, who was widowed at the beginning of war, poor lass."

"Who is the guy with them?" I heard him ask "And the other older woman?"

"Well, well! You want to know it all, don't you? Well, you'd better be prepared if you're interested in Maggie. She's here tonight with her sister and her mum 'cos they're all celebrating Maggie's engagement. The bloke that's just heading to the gents' is her new fiancé, Harry Blake."

"There you go, Mac," interjected the other man. "The lady's spoken for already, so you'd better butt out."

I felt guilty overhearing their conversation, so I looked away.

Flossie was laughing as she emptied some ashtrays and headed back to the bar. "Fiancés or even husbands never stop the Yanks, so I guess the Canucks are the same," she called behind her, grinning.

He was now walking toward me, and I vaguely remember hearing the other chap saying, "What the hell are you going to do now, Mac?"

"First, I am going to introduce myself to Maggie Graham, and for your information, Charlie, one day I'm going to marry that girl."

Did I really hear that? Well I must have done, because the whole room had obviously heard it. It suddenly went quiet, but before I had time to think about what was happening, he was standing right by our table. And, oh my, was he handsome! He took my breath away.

"Hi there, ladies," he said. "May I buy you all a drink?"

My mother looked him up and down with obvious disapproval. "We are here with a gentleman, my daughter's fiancé. Thank you for your offer, though, but we're quite alright."

My sister spoke next. But I was still speechless, staring up at him, and God help me if he wasn't staring right back at me with equal interest.

"Thank you for the offer," Beth added, gazing at the pips on his uniform, "err ... Squadron Leader, ... but we're here celebrating my sister's engagement."

"Well, congratulations, Miss Graham!" He was still looking at me. In fact, he hadn't taken his eyes off me.

"How do you know my name?" I finally spluttered.

He smiled a devastatingly handsome smile. "I'm a curious guy, so I made enquiries. My name is Cal Hamilton, by the way, and I believe you are Maggie Graham and this charming lady is your mother, Mrs. Graham, and this equally charming lady is your sister, Beth Winters."

"My goodness, you really have done your homework," said Beth, somewhat caustically. "But if you're trying to make time with my sister, you'd better get lost before Harry returns."

That was my sister, all right. A no-nonsense lady.

"I apologize for intruding on this special evening for you, Maggie, but maybe we can talk at some other time?"

I tried to be pleasant as I said, "I'm sorry, Squadron Leader Hamilton, but perhaps engagements don't mean the same in Canada as they do here in England. I have a fiancé, which means I am about to be married, so, in turn, that means you are wasting your time." I decided I could be just as scathing as my sister!

"Well, Maggie Graham, I guess I have been told in no uncertain terms! Trouble is, I think *you* might be wasting *your* time with that other fellow. You see, you and I are destined to be together."

We all laughed. "Oh really?" I replied. "Where do you get your nerve? Don't you ever give up?"

"Not with you. I never will."

His friend was now shouting his name. "Mac, leave the lady alone. Get over to the piano for god's sake and let's hear some real music. The piano player's taken a break."

I sensed he wanted to stay, even though I knew this whole act was probably just something he pulled with all women he met. Most of the Yanks at the nearby base were like this with English girls. They would flirt with them outrageously, promise them the earth and then leave them high and dry. I was smarter than to fall for that line, even though he was very attractive. In any case, I was engaged to Harry, wasn't I? I had no business finding another man attractive.

He turned and looked toward the piano. "Excuse me, ladies. I'll be right back. Maggie, please don't go away."

Harry was making his way back to our table anyway. As he sat down, he asked if the fellow had been bothering us.

"Oh no, it was fine," I replied. "Just like all those chaps at the base. Trying to chat up the girls. But between us, we put him in his place."

He started playing the piano, which really needed tuning, but his playing was magical on the keys. He played many of the favourites and soon had a receptive audience singing along. Eventually, he began to play "Just the Way You Look Tonight," and he was staring right at me. When he began to sing the words about how he would always remember the way I looked tonight, I felt myself blushing.

Everyone started clapping and calling out for more requests, but I couldn't see or hear anything but him. For some strange reason, I was completely captivated.

The regular piano player returned then, and a few couples began dancing. I saw him edging his way through the throng back to our table, and now that Harry was sitting with us, I wondered what on earth he was about to say.

When he spoke, it was the last thing I expected to hear.

"Mr. Blake," he said with considerable politeness, "might I have this dance with your fiancée?"

Harry nodded his answer, and before I knew it, I was being whisked away on the dance floor. This was all quite mad. I belonged to Harry. Yesterday, I had accepted his proposal and his ring.

Yes, it was all quite mad, but it was a magnificent madness, and somehow it seemed right.

* * *

"You have a heck of a nerve," I said, as he held me in his arms and we swayed gently to the music.

"Don't I just?"

"Harry is livid. You shouldn't have sung that song, staring at me all the time. It was very embarrassing."

"I'm sorry, but why not? It's the way I feel. I love your accent, by the way."

"You really do have a lot of nerve, Cal Hamilton. How would you feel if someone was making time with your fiancée?"

"First of all, I don't have a fiancée … yet … and secondly, I would probably punch the guy right in the face."

I laughed. "So you can see why Harry is angry."

He drew me closer. "You smell delicious, and yes, I feel very sorry for him."

"Liar! You don't feel sorry for him at all."

"How come you're engaged to him?"

"What business is that of yours?"

"You know it's my business. You don't belong with him, Maggie. Even if you didn't know that before tonight, you must know it now. Don't you feel this ... thing ... going on between us?"

"I should be angry with you, but I just think you're absolutely crazy. Completely bonkers, in fact. You've only just met me. We've hardly spoken a dozen words. There is no *thing* going on between us."

"Maggie, Maggie, Maggie, I love your choice of words. Bonkers! Yes, I'm completely and utterly bonkers about you."

He drew me even closer, and I could feel my heart beating as fast as his. "Please say you'll meet me again tomorrow."

"I'll say no such thing! I'm engaged, for heaven's sake. Can't you take a hint?"

"Nope, absolutely not. Do you live here in Grange Park?"

"Yes, well at least my Mum does, but right now I'm living in a flat in London. I work up at the War Office. Beth is home this week on leave from Portsmouth. She's in the WRENS. And Harry is ..."

"I don't want to know about Harry. I just want to know about you."

"Well, Harry is on leave, too ... but he leaves tomorrow for Didcot."

"Ah, suddenly I *do* want to hear about Harry. So he leaves tomorrow, which means you will be here alone?"

"I'm staying with Mum only until tomorrow night, and then I return to London."

"Now, isn't that the strangest of coincidences? Charlie and I are here until tomorrow too, and then we're heading up to London."

"You're full of it!"

"I'm full of love, yes. Isn't that incredible? I took one look at you, and suddenly my whole life changed."

"Like I said, you're full of it. Love doesn't happen that way, so quickly."

"And how does it happen, then? Are you in love with Harry?"

"I'm engaged to him, aren't I?"

"That's not an answer. Are you *in love* with him? And remember, you did agree to dance with me."

"I only agreed to shut you up and save an embarrassing situation, but I'm getting very angry with you now. Stop pressuring me, and take me back to the table."

"You're only angry because you know what I'm saying is true," he said, holding me even tighter. "Meet me tomorrow, Maggie, please ... or give me your address and telephone number in London."

The music suddenly stopped, and I didn't speak for a moment. We just stood there looking at each other. "I ... er ... thanks for the dance, " I said, and then rather formally I shook his hand. With that, I almost ran back across the room. I told Harry I wanted to leave, and he seemed pleased even, though he could not have guessed the reason I was so anxious to get out of there.

CHAPTER 37

CAL

I watched her walk toward the door behind her mother and sister. She was holding on tightly to Harry Blake's arm, and for a moment my heart sank. Would I ever see her again? I must have come on too strong. I had acted like a complete idiot, and yet ... I was *so* sure because it had seemed so right.

Then I looked down at my hand, which she had shaken only moments before and realized there was a crumpled piece of paper in my palm. She must have written it even before we started dancing. It simply said:

I must be crazy, but here is my address and telephone number in London. Don't make me regret this.

And there, written in pencil was all the information I needed to see her again. It was all I could do to refrain from letting out a yelp of delight to the whole pub.

I promise you, Maggie Graham, you will never regret this, I said to myself instead. *Ours will be a love story for the ages.*

* * *

I telephoned her on Monday evening, as soon as Charlie and I arrived in London. She lived in a small flat in Kensington, which she shared with another girl who was away on a course up north. Maggie invited me round for a drink. Needless to say, I did not hesitate.

Since Saturday night, I had thought of nothing but her. I had barely slept or eaten. Charlie had come to the conclusion that I was sick.

"God, man, I've never seen you like this before."

"That's because I've never been in love before, Charlie. It's damn painful, I can tell you."

"You'll feel better once you've seen her again and screwed her and then got her out of your system."

I felt like hitting him. "The feeling I have for Maggie is *not* like that, pal. I love her. I want to marry her and take her back to Canada as my wife after the war is over."

"Oh, right! Mark my words, man, you'll feel a whole lot better when you're feeling less horny."

I shook my head at him. He didn't understand. I will admit that I desired her and wanted her badly, but there was so much more. I wanted to simply sit and look at her. I wanted to talk to her, find out everything about her, her likes and dislikes, her feelings, her emotions. She had become a part of me. She was my other half, my soul mate.

"You say your name is Cal Hamilton, so why does your friend Charlie call you Mac?" was the first question she asked me, soon after I arrived at her door promptly at eight o'clock that night.

"Ah ... long story. My middle name is McBride. In my early flying days, I was always called Mac. Actually, Charlie started that. But my first name is Caleb."

"How very biblical." She grinned.

"It's a family name."

"I like Caleb or Cal better than Mac. It suits you more."

"Do I seem like a biblical guy?"

"Hardly! I just like the name."

"I like your name, too. Maggie, for Margaret, I assume?"

"Margaret Ann. And Beth is really Elizabeth. My mum felt quite proud of herself for choosing the same names as the two princesses. She used to say that the Queen copied her."

"And no doubt she treats you like two princesses, too?"

"Well, of course. Beth especially, 'cos she's had it rough since her husband Mike was killed in the Blitz in 1940. That's what made her join the WRENS. As for me, well, after I left school in 1937, I trained as a secretary, and when war was declared in 1939 I just went to work at the War Office. I'm now what they call an executive secretary to a big mucky-muck at head office. What can I get you to drink, Cal? I've only got one beer, I'm afraid. Do you like cocoa?"

"I'd drink anything you serve."

"Oh gosh, are you going to get all mushy on me again?"

I smiled. "Of course."

"Then let's get one thing straight right away. I invited you round so that you would understand. We can't start anything, Cal. I care for Harry a great deal, and—"

I interrupted her by taking her hand and pulling her into my arms. "You said the magic word. *Care* for, not *love!* That's all I needed to know. What you feel for me is something a great deal stronger, isn't it?"

She immediately took her hand away and walked over to the sofa.

"Oh Cal, why did this have to happen now? Harry is such a good man. He has pursued me faithfully for years and asked me to marry him so many times that I've lost count. I finally accepted his proposal last week, and now, suddenly you come into my life all gangbusters, talking all this romantic nonsense, and I'm so confused I don't know what to do. I can't hurt him. He's such a good man."

"You don't marry a man just because he's a good man! You marry for love. I'm nearly thirty-four years old, Maggie, and I've known many women, but I've never been in love before ... until you."

"*Known* in the biblical sense, I suppose?"

"What difference does that make? It's all in the past now."

"It makes a difference to me, Cal. I'm twenty-three and I'm still a virgin."

"Honey, I don't care if you're the Virgin Mary herself. I've fallen in love with you. Don't you get it?"

We both laughed, then, and it broke the tension between us. We sipped the warm cocoa as we sat together on the sofa, talking of everything under the sun. She was so easy to talk to, so comfortable to be with. Even the pauses in our conversation were relaxed. We just clicked. Nonetheless, we both also felt an incredible heat and passion hovering between us, and I desperately wanted to take her in my arms and make love to her. But I refused to allow myself to overwhelm her. I wanted her to feel relaxed and free of tension with me. I wanted it to be right.

"I have to be honest with Harry first," she suddenly said. "I can't go on deceiving him, telling him I have feelings for him when ... if I am seeing you."

"Ah, you do intend to keep seeing me, then?"

She flicked back that adorable strand of hair that had fallen across her forehead and covered her brown eyes, which I had just noticed had flecks of gold in them—or was that just the starlight surrounding us?

"I suppose I do."

"May I kiss you now, Maggie Graham?"

"How formal you are, Cal Hamilton."

"Well, I am a biblical guy."

We kissed then, our lips meeting gently as they had always been intended to meet, our bodies drawing closer as though they had always been one. With great restraint on my part, we didn't make love that night, even though we stayed talking and "making out" for hours like teenagers, and I finally left her at two o'clock in the morning, both of us feeling incredibly happy but sexually frustrated.

The next night I took her to dinner at the Savoy, after which we walked hand in hand back to her place. We both knew I had only one week of leave. It was wartime, and time together could be fleeting. I knew instinctively, however, that our love was not a passing fancy and we would be together forever.

She invited me inside, and this time we immediately fell into each other's arms. Kissing passionately, we headed for her bedroom, and I carried her gently to the bed. Reality seemed to be slipping away, and suddenly I felt the strongest physical and emotional desire I had ever known. My body, mind, and especially my heart ached for this woman. Her lips were trembling as we slowly took pleasure from each other's bodies and then were swept away in a torrent of emotion that took us to new heights of passion I had never thought possible.

Over the following days, we were constantly together. She even phoned in sick on two occasions, and on those days we spent the entire time in bed, loving each other with what seemed like all the passion and romance that had ever been created in the world. Like all lovers before us, we believed that no one had ever loved as we did. And by the end of that wonderful week, we were convinced that no one ever would again.

* * *

Finally, we reluctantly parted, promising to meet again at the earliest opportunity. Maggie agreed to come to Norwich the following weekend and stay near the base, so even if I was sent out on an operation she would be close by, and I would definitely head back to London on my next leave. But things were heating up on the European front now, so I wasn't sure when my next leave would be. Nonetheless, we vowed we would be together again soon.

Once back in Norwich, I wrote a quick letter to my grandmother. I told her I had met the most wonderful girl in the world and her name was Maggie and I was madly in love.

I intend to marry her and bring her home to Providence, Gran, I wrote.

The letter was very brief and to the point, and I could just imagine her smiling as she read it, probably thinking she would only believe such a thing when she saw it. Well, God willing, she would see it, because as soon as this goddamn war was over, I was taking Maggie back to

Canada. *Just stay alive until then, Granny Mac,* I willed. *Stay alive until I bring Maggie home.*

I also wrote a quick note to Letty, telling her more details about Maggie.

I know that none of you could ever believe this would happen to me, but honest to God, Letty, the moment I saw Maggie, I knew I was in love. She was the one I had been waiting for. Isn't that incredible? I can now understand how Grandad McBride felt about Granny Mac when he first saw her, and how you and Steve felt about one another. Love is the most amazing emotion, isn't it? It completely takes over your will to stay sane! But Maggie is so wonderful, and I intend to wrap myself in this insanity for the rest of my life.

I knew that would bring a smile to Letty's face, for more than anyone, she would understand the passion and depth of true love. I was sure she would confide this news to Uncle Teddy, who would also understand.

Over the coming months, Maggie and I grabbed every opportunity we could to be together, but in mid-April, strategic bombing operations in Europe had been placed under the command of General Eisenhower, who was now the Supreme Commander of the Allied Expeditionary Force, and we knew we were preparing for an Allied invasion. This meant long hours of duty.

Each time I took off on an operation now, I no longer held a fatalistic attitude about my chances of returning. Now I knew I *had* to return, because Maggie was waiting. She was my life. Without her there could be no future.

During April and May, we continued to meet when we could, and our love grew to a deep intensity as we became more and more aware of the dangers we faced. But we also knew that the war was coming to an end. The push was on in Europe, and the Allied forces in Burma were on the offensive. We were informed that about eighty per cent of German coastal radar capability had been destroyed, and on June 1, 1944, the RAF Balkan Air Force was formed to support the Yugoslavian partisans.

By then everything was in place for what would become the D-Day invasion. On the day before, Bomber Command simulated an Allied air invasion by dropping dummy paratroopers. Other simulations were carried out to perfection, and our squadrons then concentrated on the forces in the area of Caen. The news that Rome had been liberated by Allied forces caused wild celebration and led us through the next twenty-four hours on a high second to none.

D-Day finally arrived! We were one of nine squadrons of Spitfires providing cover for the fighter boys ready for the invasion of the beaches. The Allies finally had air supremacy, and things were going in our favour. The rest of June was one sortie after another, and most of the time we just felt like zombies going through the motions.

A new horror emerged on June 13, when London was attacked for the first time by the notorious V-I flying bombs, launched from sites around Pas de Calais in France. Knowing Maggie was back in London, I had a special reason to personally destroy those bombs before they reached England. Our Hawker Tempests successfully managed to destroy many of them.

By July 1, the RAF had reached its peak in strength and manpower, and by the 7th of the month we were again concentrating on enemy positions around the village of Caen. For the next few weeks, Maggie and I met only rarely. It seemed that the fates were determined to separate us. Either she was unable to get away, or when she did, I was sent off on an operation.

At the end of July, I wrote her a very formal letter asking her to marry me. She sent me back a letter asking me what had taken me so long, and yes, she would definitely marry me—any time, any place. I felt like screaming to the heavens that the most wonderful girl in the world had agreed to become my wife. I bought her a ring and we set a date: September 2, 1944, five months after we had first met. It would take that long for the formalities and legal papers to go through.

Then, in mid-August, I was suddenly given a week's leave, and we decided to spend it together in London in a swanky hotel near Hyde Park.

Not able to speed up the paperwork for our marriage, I wrote, *We'll just have to have our honeymoon before the wedding. But once the war is over and I take you back to Canada, I'll treat you to the best darned honeymoon imaginable.*

Just being with you anywhere at any time will be enough, Cal, she wrote back.

Although she had broken things off with Harry, she said she had only confided her feelings for me to him and her sister.

I couldn't wait until she was my wife and we could tell the whole damn world.

CHAPTER 38

MAGGIE

It was the best of times. It was the worst of times.

I remembered reading that at school in *A Tale of Two Cities* by Charles Dickens years ago, and I thought how ironic it was that those words suited our days together during that week in August.

It was certainly the best of times, because it was romantic and loving, and when we weren't wandering through the park holding hands, dancing close together at one of London's nightclubs to the refrain of "I'll See You Again" or our own personal song, "The Way you Look Tonight," or simply laughing at idiotic things that only seem amusing to those in love, we were together in our hotel room, which we called "our little love nest," making mad, passionate love until our bodies ached with the pure joy of being one.

How could this have happened to me? I was usually so prim and proper, and it had taken me ages to accept Harry's proposal. But with Cal, it had taken me about five minutes to know I wanted to be with him for the rest of my life. Losing my virginity to him had seemed the easiest and most obvious choice I had ever made.

But it was also the worst of times, because we were constantly interrupted by air raid warnings, bombs dropping, food shortages, and all the usual abysmal trappings of war. Nonetheless that week in August was magical for us.

"Tell me about Canada, Cal," I asked him as we lay in bed together on the last night of his leave. "I want to hear all about your family." The wireless set was playing romantic music in our room as he began to tell me more about his grandmother and about the house Providence and how he had grown up there after both his parents had died at sea.

"How sad, Cal," she whispered. "It must have been such a terrible tragedy for a little boy."

"Well, I had a great family who took care of me. A wonderful grandmother, two uncles, Letty and all the Caldwells."

And then I wanted to hear about the Caldwells, so he began at the beginning and told me how his grandfather McBride had first met Edward Caldwell. I revelled in the history of the two families.

"I know I will love Providence, Cal, and all your family, especially your grandmother, when we meet. You love her very much, don't you?" I added, "She must be very special."

"She is, Maggie." He hesitated for a moment before adding, "She was the one who gave me this."

"I've wondered about that thing you wear around your neck."

"I guess you'd call it my lucky talisman. It has certainly kept me safe through some pretty awful near-misses during these past years."

I shuddered for a moment and he kissed my forehead.

"I pray it always keeps you safe, my love," I whispered. Then I smiled. "But darling, it does scratch my boobs sometimes when we're ... you know."

He laughed. "Why didn't you ever tell me, silly girl." He took it off and placed it on the bedside table. "Tonight I will make love to you ... unadorned."

And with that we kissed passionately and began to make love with such intensity it made us both cry. I was hardly aware of Vera Lynn on the radio. I just remember those melancholy words from the song she was singing. It was called "I'll See you Again," and I prayed it would be soon.

* * *

The ringing of the telephone in our room woke us both with a sudden start. Cal gently lifted his arm stretched across me as he tried not to disturb me while looking at his watch. But I was already awake.

"God, it's only three o'clock," he said before muttering "Hello" into the phone.

I could hear Charlie's voice at the other end as Cal placed the receiver between us.

"Sorry, pal," he was saying. "I've been given the job of rounding up the troops. Something big is happening. We all have to report in today by noon. You'd better get out of that warm bed and head back up here pronto. Big op happening tonight. Better catch the first train out."

"Christ! Can't the bloody Hun at least wait one more day? I was leaving anyway tomorrow night," Cal replied.

"Quit the swearing, pal. I'm sure there's a lady present!"

"Smart-ass! Don't worry, I'm on my way." He replaced the receiver and saw me gazing up at him. He then jumped out of bed and began hunting for his pants.

"You have to go, right?"

"I'm sorry, honey. It's something big. This could be the beginning of the end, sweetheart. Peace is now in sight. And just remember, September 2nd. That day is ours, no matter what the damn Germans decide to do. I'll meet you at the church in Grange Park, just as we arranged. I'll be the guy with the flower in his lapel."

"And I'll be the one in white," I said, trying to make light of what we were both feeling.

"Start making all the plans, honey. I'll call you once I get back from this op."

"Promise?"

"I promise, my love."

I watched him as he rushed around getting dressed, checking the train timetable from Liverpool Street. I wanted to savour this moment, enjoying him.

"If I catch the first train, I'd just about make it back by noon."

Then he came back to the bed and knelt down beside me. "Always remember how much I love you, Maggie."

"I know you do, Cal. I was just practising the sound of my new name. Mrs. Caleb Hamilton."

"It sounds wonderful."

We kissed then, with such tenderness, a tenderness that would last a lifetime and into eternity. Of that I was sure.

CHAPTER 39

CAL

I arrived back at base at 11:30, which gave me just enough time for a quick shower and a spit and polish to my uniform. We then all reported to the briefing room at 12 noon precisely.

We were briefed on the importance of this mission and exactly where we would be heading in an armada of eight boxes of six squadrons each. Three hundred airmen would be taking to the air, and we were all revved to fever pitch. The weather, however, was not co-operating and by the appointed time for take-off there was still low cloud cover. So we were de-briefed, but still not allowed to leave the control room. Eventually we were briefed again, but by now there were guards posted outside to ensure no one left.

It was still a time for top secrecy. No one knew where a German spy might lurk and our operation would be uncovered. As we waited, the powers-that-be decided it might be a good plan to get us psyched up for victory, so we were all shown a film titled *Desert Victory,* which showed in graphic detail the Allies' successes in Africa. By then we were feeling pretty pumped up, but as the weather was still not co-operating, another film made in the late 1920s was brought on. It was only thirty minutes long but showed the most incredible and horrific carnage any of us had ever witnessed. It was made when the Japanese invaded China in Manchuria during that period and showed them committing unspeakable atrocities in a Chinese village. Young men were being shot to death while older men were tied to stakes and used for bayonet practice by having their stomachs split open. Young women were raped and children (kept in a pig compound) were then thrown up in the air, one at a time, to be caught on a bayonet and then thrown to another man for the same torture.

Of course we knew the reason we were being shown these horrors. If we did not hate our enemies before that film, we certainly had good reason to hate them now. We had been at war with the Germans and the Japanese for so long and had heard such terrible horror stories. Many may well have been pure propaganda, but the effect of that film shown to men going off to battle certainly had the desired effect. It was all that was needed to put us in the fighting mood for victory. But somehow, at the back of my mind, I felt sorrow for all the hate inside us. It seemed so wrong.

The weather finally cleared and the op was on. We took off, gaining height slowly in formation through the clouds above Margate in Kent and actually saw the sun appear in all its glory. It was a beautiful sight above those puffy clouds, surrounded by our armada of aircraft all hellbent on our mission for victory.

We moved quietly, as per our instructions. Any sound across our radios could alert the Hun to our position once we crossed the coastline of France. Suddenly, a novice pilot in one of the squadrons called up his leader.

"Hello, Blue Leader. This is Blue Six. Are you receiving me?"
No reply.
"Hello, Blue Leader. This is Blue Six. Are you receiving me?"
Still no reply.

The anxiety level of his voice rose in his next message. "Blue Leader, my top turret is stuck. Instructions please?"

This meant his hydraulics were obviously not working properly and he was most probably panicking and hoping for instructions to leave the formation and head home.

But there was still silence all around him.

He repeated his message three more times, by which time we were all getting very edgy and, frankly, quite irritated by this fellow for breaking our code of silence. Finally, an Australian voice cut through the silence from Red Squadron.

"For God's sake, mate, shut up, or sell the bloody plane ..."

With tension eased and no apparent adverse reaction from the Hun, we all breathed a little easier, and then someone started singing "Lily Marlene." Pretty soon we had all joined in and were singing in unison. It was a popular war song we had adopted from the Germans, and the sound of three hundred airmen singing it across the radio waves was stirring. I suddenly knew why I had been born to fly. It was exhilarating.

Underneath the lantern,
By the barrack gate,
Darling I remember
The way you used to wait.
'Twas there that you whispered tenderly,
That you loved me,
You'd always be
My Lilli of the Lamplight,
My own Lilli Marlene.

On and on we sang, disregarding the need for total silence now and convinced that our voices singing their song would rattle a few German nerves, if nothing else. We were feeling bold as we reached our assigned target and accomplished our mission in perfect order. Perhaps it made us all a little cocky, a little more relaxed. Perhaps we were not totally prepared for what happened on the way home.

As the anti-aircraft fire began attacking us, I wanted desperately to get home to Maggie, so I felt for my talisman on my neck, knowing that, despite what was happening all around me, it would surely bring me safely home.

That's when I realized I had left it on the bedside table in our hotel room in London.

CHAPTER 40

MAGGIE

I was frantic by the time I made the call to Beth.

I had already phoned everyone I could think of, but nobody would give me any information. Even my boss, who had told me that information on flight operations and safety of pilots was only given out to immediate family. Everything else was top secret.

"But I'm his fiancée," I said. "I have a right to know where he is."

"Only if you are listed as next of kin."

"But we only just got engaged. We're getting married this Saturday."

Commander Hyslop smiled as though he didn't believe me, or he'd heard that story many times before. "I'm sorry, Miss Graham," he said. "If I hear anything, I'll let you know. But you have to understand, these rules are in place for a reason. Many girls say they are engaged to American or Canadian airmen but …"

"Well, I'm not *many girls!*" I raised my voice. "My mother and my sister know I am engaged, and they are planning my wedding as we speak."

"I really am sorry—"

I didn't let him continue. I just ran out of his office, slamming the door behind me. Back in the typing pool, I picked up my handbag and jacket and headed back to my flat, where I called Beth again at Mum's house. I was sure she must have arrived from Portsmouth by now.

She picked up at the first ring.

"Oh Beth, thank God you're there. I don't know what to do. Cal never phoned me after his last op. He left Sunday night, and I've heard nothing since. No one will tell me anything because I'm not next of kin. What can I do?" I was sobbing into the phone.

"I'm sure he's okay, Mags. He'll make it for the wedding on Saturday."

"But he promised to phone me when he got back from that operation. Supposing he—supposing he was killed?"

"Look, sit tight, I'm catching the next train up to London and will be with you in a couple of hours. It will all be okay, sweetheart, I promise."

I fell into her arms when she finally arrived at my door at about six o'clock. "I've still heard nothing, Beth. I know he would have got in touch by now."

"Look, love, it's going to be all right, I'll find out something for you through the base. I'm staying here with you now, as I took my week's leave from today instead of Friday. I'll make some tea first, and we can sit and work this out together."

"I don't want bloody tea, Beth. I want to know Cal is safe."

"I know love, I know."

She kept hugging me and patting my back and then finally got up and put the kettle on. Suddenly, there was a knock on the door. I jumped up and flung it open. A man in uniform stood there, but it wasn't Cal. I felt my heart collapse inside my body. This couldn't be happening. I knew the moment I saw this man's face that it must be bad. His expression was grim.

"Are you Maggie Graham?" the stranger asked.

I nodded.

"My name is Peter; you might have heard of me as Peg. I'm a friend of your fiancé, Cal Hamilton."

"Oh God, is he okay? Please tell me he's all right."

"May I come inside, Maggie?"

I think Beth took over then. She opened the door wider and directed the man into my apartment. She held me tightly as the man began to speak.

"I promised Cal I would find you if ... But I'm sorry it took me so long. I couldn't get leave until this afternoon."

"Tell me. What happened?" My voice broke.

"I'm so sorry—his plane was shot down over France."

"Did he bail out?"

"I'm afraid he didn't survive, Maggie."

"NO! NO! NO!" I think I was screaming.

I don't recall what happened next. All I remember was that the kettle kept on whistling, and this stranger and Beth were crying.

I then fell into a black hole where I could make-believe this had never happened.

CHAPTER 41

JANE (Victoria)

They all kept hovering around me. It was most annoying. I'm sure they meant well, but didn't they realize it was just making things worse?

I had been sitting in the drawing room writing a letter to Caleb when the telegram arrived. I knew what it said even before Teddy read it to us all. He was gone. Our dear, sweet Caleb was gone. *Killed in action*, the telegram said.

They had given me a shot of brandy, and now Teddy kept saying he wanted to give me a sedative to make me sleep. I didn't want a sedative, and I didn't want to sleep. It was barely six o'clock in the evening, and I wanted to keep a clear head. The brandy had been more than enough.

Poor Letty was crying, and her eyes were now red and swollen. Dear soul that she was, always comforting and giving solace to everyone. How this must hurt her, for Caleb had been like the child she never had, or at least another younger brother to her.

But it was me that they kept fussing over. "Poor Granny Mac," they whispered. "How will she bear this at her age?" I could hear them talking quite clearly.

I wanted to scream at them all!

"My hearing hasn't gone yet! I know what you're all saying. At my age, indeed! Don't you all realize I'm made of stronger stuff than any of you?"

I was ninety-nine years old when the telegram arrived at Providence, so I knew it wouldn't be long before I would be with them all again anyway, those who had left me through the years. My little Caleb so long ago, my beloved Gideon, my dearest Sarah and her

Ernest, dear Edward, my dear friend Dulcie who had passed away last year at a hundred and two, and now my grandson Caleb.

Oh damn you, Caleb McBride Hamilton, why did you have to die before me, too? Those darn air machines. I told you years ago they would be the death of you!

"Mother, I think it would be best if you take this sedative, and it will help you sleep right through the night," Teddy repeated once again.

"Teddy, I told you before, I don't need it. The brandy was fine. Now stop hovering around me, all of you. I want to sit and think for a while with a clear head. Then Letty can take me upstairs to my room, in the elevator."

Imagine, Caleb! Last year we had an elevator installed at Providence alongside the servants' staircase at the back of the house. Did I tell you that in a letter already? I can't remember. But my old legs wouldn't take me up the stairs anymore, and for a while they brought my bed down to the library and I slept there, but now I ride up in the elevator like a queen every night and I can sleep in my own room once again.

"All right, Granny Mac." That was Letty fussing now. "But can I get you something to eat? I'll tell Mrs. Potter to go ahead and prepare us all some supper now, shall I? We could all do with a bite."

"Oh Letty, dear, stop fussing. Potter can just make us a salad or something light if it would make you happy, but meanwhile I want you, Teddy, to stop behaving like my doctor, and you, Letty, to stop being my nurse. I shall be fine, so let's just act like a family instead. We'll talk about Caleb for a while. It will do us good to talk about him ..." I let my words trail off.

Bertie sat down then. He had been pacing back and forth as though he imagined I was about to collapse in a heap or have a heart attack. *Well, I'll surprise them all! You always called me a tough old gal, didn't you Caleb?*

They all let out a collective sigh of relief that old Granny Mac was going to get through this after all.

One at a time, we began to talk about Caleb and all that he had meant to each of us. We remembered him as that dear, sweet, small boy who had those terrible nightmares after his parents were gone. We recalled his passion for flying as a young man. His barnstorming days, and how crazy he was doing those ridiculous stunts, and how he conned us all into allowing him to delay going to Oxford for a few years. We even managed to laugh a little. We also remembered his many contributions to the McBride business before he left for Europe and that beastly war.

"God only knows what will happen now, Mother. I always imagined young Cal taking over completely from me, once he came back from the war."

"They never seem to come back ..." whispered Letty as she took my hand in hers. She was taking this harder than any of us.

Mrs. Potter called us into the drawing room then, and we tried valiantly to eat her potato salad and some salad greenery from the garden. *Rabbit food, Cal called it.*

"He always wanted to fly. It was his life," I said, as we all sat down.

"So at least he died doing what he loved doing best," added Letty.

"But so young," said Teddy. "Far, far too young."

We then talked of a memorial service for him at St. Luke's, and the twins said they would arrange it all for me.

By eight o'clock, I was very tired and I beckoned for Letty to assist me up to bed. Once in my room, she helped me prepare for bed. We prayed together, as we did every night, but on that particular night, we prayed especially for Caleb, that he might find eternal peace.

It was only when I was alone, tucked up under the covers, that I allowed the tears to flow.

* * *

We held a memorial service on September 10, 1944, which would have been Caleb's thirty-fourth birthday. The church was full to capacity.

I insisted on going up the trail through our own property to St. Luke's instead of by car along the road. I knew I would never be able to walk the trail, even with the aid of my cane, so they put me in my wheelchair and Teddy and Bertie took turns wheeling me there. They both read Lessons, and Letty managed, through her tears, to deliver a perfect eulogy. She also honoured Caleb's friend, Charles Fuller, who had been killed on the same day as Caleb, along with ten other pilots from throughout the Commonwealth. She read out all their names with deep emotion.

We made arrangements for Caleb's headstone to be placed alongside those of Sarah, Ernest and Steve. *One complete family all gone*, I thought.

So the McBrides and the Hamiltons are all gone now. I'm the only one left, and I won't be here for much longer. Bertie and Teddy are still here, of course, but there is no hope of them continuing our lineage now. Far too old. Well, at least the Caldwells were prolific, and they will go on ... not through Letty, though. Dear girl, she never did marry that fellow Austin. So loyal to Stephen's memory.

My thoughts kept rambling on that way. Caleb's death seemed to make me more confused, and very forgetful, too. I kept getting people's names mixed up. Sometimes I even forgot faces. This disturbed me a great deal. I had never been like this before.

I think it was sometime in late October or early November when I received a strange letter from an English woman named Beth Winters. The letter also confused me for some reason. It came at the time I was receiving so many letters of condolence, but I was sure I didn't know anyone named Beth Winters. And who was Maggie Graham?

Was I becoming senile? Losing my memory? Hadn't Caleb mentioned a girl called Maggie once? He said he had fallen in love? Or was that Steve? Or Sarah? I couldn't seem to sort things out as clearly as I once could.

I read the letter through twice.

Dear Mrs. McBride:

You don't know me, but my sister, Maggie, and I knew your grandson, Caleb Hamilton, in England. I now wish to send you my deepest condolences on his passing. Actually my sister does not know I am writing to you and would not wish me to convey what I am about to tell you, but I am doing it anyway because I feel it is my duty to let you know the truth.

Your son and Maggie were very much in love and had intended to marry on September 2nd this year. Four days earlier, he was killed in action. My sister was devastated, and I doubt she will ever fully recover from her grief.

There is something, however, that you, as Cal's grandmother, have the right to know. One month after Cal's death, Maggie discovered she was pregnant. She is carrying his child and the baby is due next May.

Maggie intends to raise this child on her own, so please don't think I am writing to you for assistance. She is a proud woman and is simply happy in the knowledge that Cal will live on in this child that she will bear. My only wish is that this news might bring you some joy, knowing that your grandson left a part of him behind.

Please forgive me for intruding on your family's grief, but I thought you should know.

Sincerely, Beth Winters.

I put the letter aside. I think I placed it in my special box with all my journals the last time they carried me up to the turret. I would deal with it later, but it kept nagging at me.

Could it be true? Or was this woman just clever? Looking for a handout? Maybe it wasn't Caleb's child at all that her sister was carrying?

I'd heard that so many English women claimed to be pregnant by the Americans or Canadians during wartime and it wasn't always true.

But that name—Maggie? It rang a bell, somehow. *Oh, why won't my memory work properly these days? Maybe I should talk with the boys and Letty about it later. Letty would know what to do, for sure. Or I could read through Cal's letters to me again and find out if he mentioned a Maggie.*

But time and days all seemed to pass in a blur, and pretty soon it was Christmas and I had all but forgotten about the letter. We had so much snow in Victoria that year and we were all housebound for a long time. I recalled the times when dear Ah Foo was with us and how much he had enjoyed clearing the snow. The white stuff always made him happy. Looking out through my bedroom window, I could still picture him down there, playing in it like a foolish child. Why was it that I could clearly recall such events from so long ago, and yet I became confused by more recent events?

Occasionally, something popped into my mind about a letter I should answer, but no sooner had it popped in than it jumped right out again. Letty had attended to all my correspondence answering the letters of condolence, so maybe she had answered it. *I'll ask her later,* I thought. But then I forgot.

Toward the end of May, in the spring of 1945, just as all the new beauty of Providence was once again beginning to blossom, another letter came from England for me. It was from that same woman, Beth Winters, and it was short and to the point:

"Dear Mrs. McBride:
Following on my letter of last October, I thought you would wish to know that my sister, Maggie, gave birth to a daughter on May 13th, 1945. Her name is Victoria Jane Blake, and she is a healthy child. I assure you that her biological father was your grandson, Cal Hamilton.
My sister, however, married Harry Blake in January of this year, not I might add because her love for Cal had lessened, but because Harry Blake

*is a good man who has loved her for many years and wished to help her
raise her daughter as his.*

*Again, I am going against the wishes of both my sister and her husband.
But for Cal's sake, and for the baby's, I thought you at least should know the
truth. Do with it what you will. My sister does not need any financial help,
if that is what you might be thinking, for Harry is quite able to take care
of her and her child. But Cal would want you to know the truth, I'm sure.*

Sincerely, Beth Winters."

I at least should know the truth, she said! *Oh what a burden to place
on an old woman,* I thought. What should I do? Could it be true? She
did not appear to want anything from us financially. She just thought
it important that I should know the truth.

I wrestled with this truth all summer, but I kept this knowledge
to myself. By September, my mind seemed much clearer. A whole year
had passed since Caleb's death, and his birthday had come around
again. Did he have a daughter in England? Could it be true? How could
I make it right? I would be one hundred years old at Christmas, and
the family intended to celebrate the event in style.

Supposing I didn't make it? I could go at any time. And then this
child, this little girl in England, would never know her true parentage,
just as I had never known mine until Gideon found the truth for me.
Oh, maybe her aunt would tell her. But maybe not. Her new father,
Harry Blake, might never allow the truth to come out. Could I let that
happen?

I knew only too well how it felt never to know the truth about
your parentage. Finally, I decided that would not happen to Caleb's
daughter.

CHAPTER 42

"Letty, do you remember Caleb mentioning a girl in England he had met shortly before he died?" I asked her one day in early October.

She smiled. "Yes, I certainly do. He said he was madly in love with her. I was a little sceptical, I must admit, knowing Cal's track record with the ladies. But, if he mentioned her to you too, he must have been serious. I don't remember him writing again after that. Things were heating up in Europe by then."

"What was her name?"

"The girl? Maggie, I think," she replied.

"That's what I thought too. Now, I want to see one of your lawyer brothers—either William or John?"

She looked at me with her head tilted. "Is it about a legal matter, Granny Mac?"

"Yes, dear, it is. Now, ask one of them to come over and bring with him a copy of my Will. I think I might add something."

"Of course. I'll attend to it for you."

William Caldwell, her older brother, arrived the next morning promptly at ten o'clock and was brought into the den, where I was waiting for him.

"First of all, William," I began, "I want you to know that I am now quite sound of mind and understand exactly what I'm about to do."

"Well, of course, Granny Mac. I never doubted that."

"Some people might. At nearly a hundred, people think you've lost all your marbles!"

He laughed. He was a nice fellow, and I liked him. All the Caldwells were nice people. "Now, what can I do for you?"

"What I am about to do is to be kept strictly between you and me, and is to remain that way in confidence until my will is read after my death, which probably won't be much longer now. You see, I want to add a codicil to the will, but it's not to take effect until after both Bertie and Teddy have also passed on. Is that possible?"

"Absolutely—if that is your wish."

"Providence is to remain their home until they die and all my estate goes to them, as my will dictates. All the other bequests in my will also remain the same."

He nodded.

"But, following Bertie and Teddy's deaths, this house and my entire fortune is to pass to one Victoria Jane Blake, so long as she has by then attained the age of twenty-one."

He raised one eyebrow. "May I ask who Victoria Jane Blake is?"

"No, you may not! But in this other envelope, which is to remain sealed until after the deaths of both of my sons, there will be the explanation for her right to my property."

He started to make notes.

"Is all that perfectly clear, William?"

"Yes, it is, although I will need more than just a name if she is a beneficiary. I will need an address, so that she can be notified at the appropriate time."

"There is a current address on the back of this envelope. Use that one, and when the time comes for her to inherit, twenty or thirty years from now, after the twins pass on, I daresay you clever lawyers and your private investigators will be able to track her down."

"This Victoria Jane Blake is still an infant then, I presume?"

"Don't presume anything, William. And don't ask any more questions. Just get it all typed up and bring it back for me to sign as soon as possible. Understood?"

"I understand." He stood up, took my hand in his and kissed it gallantly.

The Caldwells were always such perfect gentlemen.

* * *

Two days later, he returned with my will, and the codicil had been added as I had instructed. I signed my name to it and handed him the sealed envelope, which contained the letters from Beth Winters telling of this child's birth. I also gave him another letter I had written addressed to Victoria Jane Blake, which was only to be opened by her once she inherited the house. He placed everything with my will.

I felt better then. The deed was done. It was the best thing I could think of in the circumstances, and the only way to play out the scenario to its end. Sarah always said I liked to organize people's lives, and maybe she was right.

Well, that's as may be, but this was still the right way to do it—perhaps the only way. It would enable my boys to live out their lives comfortably at Providence, but it would also ensure that the dynasty did not come to an end after they were gone. If this child, Victoria Jane Blake, really is Caleb's daughter, then she would inherit the property, but only if she agrees to live here. The house must never be sold.

I wondered if that might be a little strong—to expect someone to move from their own country as an adult into a strange house in a foreign country. I was sure she *would* by then be an adult, because Bertie and Teddy would hopefully live for many more years.

But was I playing God? What would this knowledge do to a child if she had never been told about her true parentage? Perhaps this would place her mother, Maggie, and the man who raised her, Harry Blake, into turmoil.

I wrestled with my thoughts long after William Caldwell had left with the signed will and codicil to store in his vault. The deed was finally done, and I decided I would now simply place the whole problem in the hands of God. If it was meant to be, it would all work out. *What is to be will be,* I told myself. *If it is God's plan, everything will work out as it should. Destiny will take care of it. I'm much too old to worry about it all now.*

"Letty," I called out.

She ran in from the kitchen, where she had been helping Mrs. Potter with the menu for that night. "What can I do for you, Granny Mac?"

"I want to play the piano again for a while."

"But your hands, dear. Aren't they still a little stiff?"

"Just a tad, but I won't be playing for long. Then I want you to help me upstairs to my room. After that, if the twins are home, I would like them to come up too, and carry me up to the turret."

"Whatever for?"

"Mind your business, young lady! I simply want to sit up there and look out over the grounds toward the mountains, that's all. Haven't done that in a long while. Gideon and I always sat up there together, you know."

"All right, dear. I'll help you to the drawing room to play, first."

"Em, no, I think I'll play on this old piano today. It's the one Gideon gave me on our wedding day, you know. It came all the way around the Horn."

"Yes, Granny Mac, I know," she said patiently, having heard that story many times.

I began to play some of my favourite Chopin, but she was right, my fingers were stiff. *Darned arthritis.*

After a while, I stopped.

"Shall I call Uncle Bertie and Uncle Teddy now? I think they are both home this morning."

"Good girl."

Letty then took me up in the elevator to my bedroom, and the boys followed us up. They then joined crossed hands for me to sit on the cradle they made and then they struggled up the narrow, spiral staircase to the turret.

"Good job you're just a lightweight, Mother," Bertie said, chuckling. They were such dear boys, and I was so proud of them both.

They sat me in my rocking chair up there, and Letty fussed around with blankets because it was a little cool.

"Thank you all, my dears. Now, you can leave me for an hour. I want to sit here by the window and watch the world go by—and think about how fortunate I am."

"I don't want you to catch a chill, dear," said Letty. "So I'll be back in an hour for you."

They climbed back down the stairs then and went about their business, and I was finally alone.

I loved the silence. The room still smelled of Gideon's pipe and his masculine aroma. Or was it my imagination? Was he close by me?

I took out my journal and began to write an entry for the day, October 5th, 1945.

This may well be my last entry, I began. I then wrote a lot of meaningful things about my wonderful family and how very lucky I had been. I wrote about Gideon and Sarah and the twins, and about my infant son, Caleb, and then about my dear grandsons, Stephen and Caleb.

How blessed I have been. Little Jane Hopkins, orphan, to have lived so long in such a wonderful place and to have been so loved. Could anyone really ask for more?

Suddenly I began to feel very tired, but I knew I still had things to do.

I continued writing. *Once I finish this final entry, I will unlock my oak chest and place my journal inside, along with all the others. I will place the broken half of Gideon's talisman in the musical box he gave me so long ago. I stopped wearing it after Caleb was killed, because his half hadn't protected him and brought him back to me after all. I will then place the box and my very first gift from Mr. Lloyd with the pressed flowers inside.* I paused in thought and then continued writing. *"Maybe I should never have broken the talisman in two? But then, hadn't I always known that he and I would not meet again in this world? It was just that I had thought I would be the one to go first. But what of the two halves? I still believe that destiny will join them together again one day. How would that happen now, I wonder?*

Maybe I will never know. Maybe we are not meant to know what will happen in the future. It's God's plan, not ours. It reminds me of something I once read in a book called The Prophet, by Kahlil Gibran, with a chapter about children. I recall it by heart:

"You may give them your love, but not your thoughts, for they have their own thoughts. You may house their bodies but not their souls, for their souls dwell in the House of Tomorrow which you cannot visit, not even in your dreams."

It is true. I must trust that the future will unravel the way it should. I have had my life, and I can no longer be a part of the children's lives in the future. I just hope that their House of Tomorrow will be happy, just as mine has been.

But for now ... my own story ends."

* * *

Jane closed the musical box and placed it back in the oak chest, along with her journals, her letters, the talisman and her jewellery, locking everything safely away. She then attached the key to the key ring and placed it in the drawer of the table beside her. The exertion had made her short of breath, so she leaned back and closed her eyes for a while.

Suddenly, she was sure she could hear beautiful music playing far off in the distance. Someone was playing the piano. It was a piece by Beethoven, and it sounded so peaceful. Perhaps she saw her beloved

Gideon holding out his hand to her, leading her towards that peaceful place where the music was playing. It would be nice to imagine that was the way her story ended.

An hour later, they found her there. Jane Hopkins McBride had fallen into her last eternal sleep. Her Bible was in her lap. A slight smile appeared to cross her lips. Letty closed her eyes for the last time as she and her two sons sobbed their final farewells.

The following day, her obituary ran in the local newspaper.

McBride, Jane Hopkins Sheridan. Passed peacefully
into the arms of her Lord on October 5th, 1945.
Mrs. McBride was the widow of Captain Gideon McBride, a pioneer
Fraser River Boat Captain in the 1850s and 1860s,
who predeceased her in 1898. McBride's
Transportation is still well known in this province as
it has continued to diversify and grow through the years
into the canning, airways, and tourism industries.
Mrs. McBride first arrived in the colony aboard the
Tynemouth in 1862, and is one of this city's longest
living and best-known pioneers.
Mrs. McBride was also predeceased by an infant
son, Caleb, in 1869, a grandson, Stephen Hamilton,
killed in action in 1916, a daughter, Sarah, and
son-in-law, Ernest, who lost their lives aboard
the ill-fated Princess Sophia in 1918, and another
grandson, Caleb McBride Hamilton in 1944, killed in
action while serving his country in Europe.
Mrs. McBride was well known for her benevolence
to numerous charities including the poor, the
homeless and the Indigenous people and has
donated a great deal of her money to funding
Musical Societies and Scholarships

throughout British Columbia and in England.
She is survived by her twin sons, Albert and
Edward, who will miss her dearly, as will her
extended Caldwell family, especially Letitia Ann
Caldwell, as well as her many friends.
Mrs. McBride will be buried alongside her
husband in the McBride family plot in the cemetery
at St. Luke's-Church-On-The-Hill, a church she
and her late husband helped to build on land they
donated. A service will be conducted there at 11 a.m.
on Sunday, October 14th.
Donations in the name of Jane Hopkins Sheridan McBride
may be made to any of the charities to which
Mrs. McBride had dedicated her long life.

EPILOGUE

WILLIAM CALDWELL

The day after the funeral, as we sat in the drawing room at Providence, I looked around the room at all their dear, familiar faces.

Yesterday, after the reception, I had gone back to my office. For the longest time, I sat thinking as I fingered the envelope containing Jane McBride's Last Will and Testament, together with the other sealed letter she had given me, which could not be opened by this mysterious person in England until after the deaths of the McBride twins.

Soon I would read the will for her family, and I knew they would all benefit greatly from her generosity. I would also include the codicil and tell them about a letter which could not yet be opened. They would all wonder, and I would have to explain her instructions to me.

The twins were only in their early seventies, so, by the law of averages, they could both live into their nineties. By then, this unknown infant in England could be in her twenties. I might be gone too by then, so it may well be the responsibility of another lawyer in the firm to carry out these wishes. But I hope it will still be me, because I really want to see how this will all pan out and who this mysterious person is.

I was sure there would be many questions from the family, but I really know nothing more than that Granny Mac had decided to leave her house and the rest of her fortune to someone in England that none of us knew. All she told me was that it would continue the McBride family story into tomorrow. One day in the far distant future, the puzzle will be solved.

No point in speculating today. All I could do was my duty as the family's lawyer to honor the connection and long-time friendship between the Caldwells and the McBrides.

But I would love to know how it turns out one day.

The other envelope, to be opened by that person who would inherit Providence, had been placed in the McBride safety deposit box, locked safely away until that far distant tomorrow.

And now, as they all sat waiting, I cleared my throat and began reading.

THE END

The McBride Chronicles continue in Book Four: *Tomorrow*

MUSIC MENTIONED IN THE BOOK:

(Credited as follows)
"They Can't Take That Away From Me" by George Gershwin with lyrics by Ira Gershwin, 1936.
"The Way You Look Tonight" by Jerome Kern, 1936.
"I'll See You Again," by Noel Coward, 1929.
"Lily Marlene," lyrics by Hans Leip, 1915. Music by Norbert Schultze, 1938

ACKNOWLEDGMENTS

Once again I have many people to thank and acknowledge for helping me with Book THREE in the McBride Chronicles Series.

In *Legacy* I have included stories of both world wars and the effect they had on the people back home in Victoria, British Columbia, Canada. In addition I thank the Victoria Maritime Museum for history research on the sinking of the *S.S. Sophia*.

In respect to the two world war histories, I want to thank and honour all those special young men who fought in the First World War and left their stories behind for researchers like myself to be able to fully understand the horror of those times. I especially honour my own family hero in WWI, an uncle, Eric Stofer, who was killed in France just two weeks before Armistice Day in 1918. I have taken the liberty of using part of his story to describe Stephen's life in *Legacy*. Although it is vastly different in many ways (because Eric joined up to fight for king and country from England and died two years after Stephen did), I have used one of Eric's letters written to his older sister, Nell, for part of Stephen's letter to his mother.

For stories from World War II, I again honor all those who served, including my own father. For more RCAF information, I consulted with an old friend of my father's, the late John Betts, who served as a bomber pilot during the war. He was an Englishman who came to Canada to train pilots back east but was then recruited by the RAF to return to England and form a squadron. His adventures and those of his squadron enabled him to share with me many incredible stories of the hair-raising adventures he had between 1941 and 1945. He was one of the lucky ones who survived and came home safely to share those tales with the next generation.

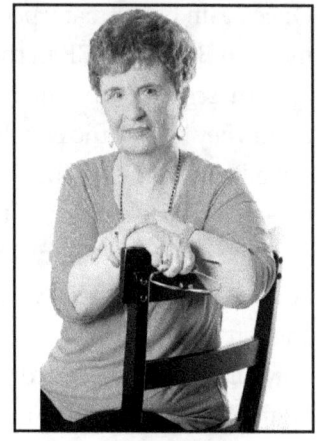

I am so grateful to him for sharing these memories, many of which I have adapted for Cal's story. These men were brave beyond all reason, but "Bomber Betts," as he was fondly called, told me on many occasions, "we weren't particularly brave because we were all just scared stiff and a little bit crazy." I hope I have adequately portrayed both their bravery and their craziness, which helped to defeat evil and win the war.

I am also indebted to many other writers and researchers who covered these periods in history before me and helped with my own research.

And many thanks once again to the Hancock House team.

I acknowledge and am honoured to have placed my fictitious house Providence on the unceded Coast Salish territory of the Lekwungen First Nation people in Victoria, British Columbia.

ABOUT THE AUTHOR

Valerie Green was born in England and studied journalism, short-story writing and English literature at the Regent Institute of Journalism in London. She aspired to being a writer since she was a child and has always been passionate about history. Before immigrating to Canada in 1968, Valerie's employment included a short stint at the War Office for MI5, as well as legal secretarial work and freelance writing. Her writing career is extensive and includes writing a weekly history column for the *Saanich News* for nineteen years, a monthly column for the Seaside Times in Sidney, BC, for ten years, articles for the Victoria Times Colonist, as well as authoring over twenty books on local and regional history, mysteries and social issues. Now semi-retired, Valerie reviews books for British Columbia Reviews and freelances for newspapers and magazines. She lives with her husband in Saanich, BC, on Vancouver Island.

Visit her website at www.valeriegreenauthor.com
Contact her at hello@valeriegreenauthor.com

THE MCBRIDE CHRONICLES

VALERIE GREEN

VALERIE GREEN

Providence
a novel
THE McBRIDE CHRONICLES
BOOK ONE

Destiny
a novel
THE McBRIDE CHRONICLES
BOOK TWO

VALERIE GREEN

VALERIE GREEN

Legacy
a novel
THE McBRIDE CHRONICLES
BOOK THREE

Tomorrow
a novel
THE McBRIDE CHRONICLES
BOOK FOUR

This four-book series spans through six generations of two families, from the 1840s to present day. Strong women characters who overcome incredible odds are included in each of the four books, intertwined with real historical events through British Columbia and Canada.

Hancock House Publishers
19313 0 Ave, Surrey, BC V3Z 9R9
www.hancockhouse.com
sales@hancockhouse.com
1-800-938-1114